A DANGEROUS THING

A DANGEROUS
THING

Sarah Harrison

severn
House

This first world edition published in Great Britain 2002 by
SEVERN HOUSE PUBLISHERS LTD of
9–15 High Street, Sutton, Surrey SM1 1DF.
This first world edition published in the USA 2002 by
SEVERN HOUSE PUBLISHERS INC of
595 Madison Avenue, New York, N.Y. 10022.

British Library Cataloguing in Publication Data

Harrison, Sarah, 1946–
  A dangerous thing
  1. Suspense fiction
  I. Title
  823.9′14 [F]

ISBN 0-7278-5810-6

Typeset by Palimpsest Book Production Ltd.,
Polmont, Stirlingshire, Scotland.
Printed and bound in Great Britain by
MPG Books Ltd., Bodmin, Cornwall.

Preface

You're about to read my very first – and previously unpublished – novel. I wrote it over thirty years ago when I was in my early twenties, newly married and pregnant.

Since leaving university I'd worked first on *Woman's Own* and then gone freelance to concentrate on what was always my first love, fiction. Back then this consisted wholly of magazine short stories. I knew my market and was learning a lot about my craft. Over a period of a year my output and my success rate steadily increased. I realised that I could no longer put off attempting a novel. But I also knew the pitfalls that await the unwary first-time novelist striving for searing honesty and emotional truth: I was determined not to be autobiographical.

It was only when I came to re-read *A Dangerous Thing* to prepare it for this Severn House edition that I realised to what spirited (some would say foolhardy) lengths I went to avoid the slough of self-indulgence. 'Write about what you know'? I don't think so. For, so far from being an in-depth study of the marital relationships of impecunious young professionals in Paddington's flat land, this is a noirish time-slip thriller set in rural Devon, with a complex, male – first-person, forsooth – perspective. Plus premonitions, prejudice, trial by tabloid, suicide and murder.

I set myself a challenge, alright, but I'm glad that I did. I've always believed that for writers 'what we know' has more to do with the human condition and our knowledge of feelings, moods and sensibilities than with how we spend our time. Imagination can create story, characters and background: personal experience breathes life into them.

I cut my literary teeth on this novel, but a good story can stand the test of time, and *A Dangerous Thing* remains a good story.

Sarah Harrison

One

The first few slow tears of rain trickled down the windscreen as I drove into Ballacombe. It was five thirty on a late August afternoon but the sky, bruised with storm clouds, and now the rain, made it seem dark and autumnal. The wide main street of the village was deserted. A few unseasonal lights shone from uncurtained front rooms but, other than that, my first impression was of a pervasive, closed greyness.

I drove slowly, an intruder, peering through the rain to right and left to get my bearings. I was not bothered about inconveniencing other traffic, for there was none. My noisy old Morris might have been a creature from another age or planet as it chugged through the deepening puddles. Frustrated, I pulled into the side of the road and fished in my coat pocket for the map Tyrrell had given me with directions to the cottage. Typically, in his efforts to be helpful he had well-nigh submerged the outlines of roads in a forest of notes in red biro. These notes, designed to clarify things but actually doing the reverse, were as chatty and uneconomical as the man who'd written them, containing remarks like: 'This section not to scale, it's actually longer than the first stretch of road but don't be put off, keep going till you reach the pub, then fork left.' This was followed by a large arrow, abundantly feathered and curlicued – I could imagine Tyrrell's well-chewed biro weaving idly about while his concentration, ever a fragile flower, wafted away in a daydream. The rest was just as bad. I had by my own efforts got as far as Ballacombe High Street but I was dependent on the eccentricities of the map from now on.

The light was getting worse as the rain became heavier and Tyrrell had not indicated whether I should be leaving the village to the north or south. Feeling that any action was better than none, I started the engine and curb-crawled down the street, keeping my eyes peeled for someone to ask. But these hardy country folk were too shrewd to be caught out in the rain, I thought cynically.

Passing a narrow road leading off to the left, I saw that it led to the village church, its sturdy Norman tower like a thumbs up in the pessimistic rain. A light was on inside and, as I watched, a figure emerged, having turned the light off, and threaded swiftly through gravestones towards the road. Under the canopy of the lychgate he stopped for a moment, bunching up the skirts of his cassock, and then came on in my direction. It was the vicar, huddled beneath a voluminous oilskin cape like a policeman's.

I rolled down the window and called: 'Excuse me, could you help me?'

'Of course.' He ran over with that comical knock-kneed gait that women have when they run in a skirt, and put his face down to the window. The face was red and friendly, like a storybook farmer's, with curly grey hair plastered to his brow by the rain.

'Thanks,' I said. 'Look.' I produced Tyrrell's map, twisting it around to try and indicate what I considered must be my position on it. My irritation must have been apparent for he laughed and said affably: 'Never mind about that – where do you want to get to?'

'I don't know whether you'll know it – Rook's Cottage, Horsfall Lane.'

'Oh yes. Robert Tyrrell's place.'

'You know him?'

'Only slightly, but he comes down from time to time – a very likeable chap.'

'He's a colleague of mine at London University, he's lent me the place for a few months.'

The rain suddenly came down harder, hissing meanly on the pavement and roaring on the roof of the car. The vicar said: 'Look, I know where it is. Perhaps you could drop me off at Glebe House at the bottom of the hill and I'll direct you from there.'

'Fine.' I pushed open the door and he climbed in, the massive folds of the streaming cape seeming to fill the small car. I started the engine. 'Incidentally,' I said, 'my name's Michael Bowater.'

'Cyril Thorne, nice to meet you. Don't go too fast, the Glebe's just at the bottom, here on the left.' A few hundred yards further on he motioned me to stop.

'Now,' he said, 'press on along this road for about another mile till you get to a pub, the Lamb and Flag. Fork left, then first right and it's up on your right. The last turning's not much more than a cart track really, it doesn't lead anywhere, but don't be put off – it's perfectly passable and the cottage isn't far up.'

'God.'

'You won't need His help, I promise you.' He grinned.

'I'm sorry.'

'Forget it. I understand your misgivings but it's not as bad as it sounds.'

'Thanks so much.'

'A pleasure. If you look at Mr Tyrrell's map again in the light of what I've told you, you'll see it contains most of the salient points. Now – would you like to come in for some tea? Or a glass of sherry?'

The prospect was inviting, Glebe House was solid, square, painted white, showing up bright and friendly in the downpour. But I knew if I didn't get to this damn cottage soon the settling in would be even worse. Delay might be fatal to the enterprise.

'There's nothing I'd like better. It's awfully good of you, but I feel I ought to get there and get unpacked.'

'I understand, Another time perhaps. I'm bound to bump into you in the village – and now you know where we are, I can rely on you to knock on the door?'

'I will. Thanks again.'

'*Au revoir*, then.' Thorne got out, allowing an explosion of wind and rain into the car, gathered his cape about him and began to run up the path to the house. Lucky man, returning to a cosy hearth, a home-cooked meal and, doubtless, a charming wife on this filthy evening. Enviously I watched him open the door and wipe his sodden shoes for a moment before closing it after him.

With a sigh I started up the engine. Stiffen the sinews, summon up the blood. I had elected to come, I must meet the challenges of rural life with fortitude.

The vicar's instructions, allied with the now miraculously clear map, were sound and I was gratified to see the Lamb and Flag looming through the murk after only another five minutes driving. I forked left between tall banks and slowed down, looking out for the turning to Rook's Cottage. When I did come upon it I almost turned round and headed back to the vicarage. It was indeed no more than a cart track, not a very recently used one at that, and rapidly turning to a mire under the onslaught of the rain. The red Devonshire mud was being diluted into something akin to tomato soup in the deep ruts and the wheels of the Morris began to spin and churn hopelessly. I rolled the window down and looked about me. There was the cottage a little way ahead on the right. I considered the possibility of getting out, salvaging the more manoeuvrable items among my luggage and making a run for it, but as if to chastise me for my stupidity the rain gave vent to a burst like machine-gun fire and I hastily rolled the window back up.

After another abortive attempt to proceed, I realised that I was not entirely stuck. The car would not go forward but was rolling back quite easily. I decided to take a run at it. I reversed back into the lane until my exhaust was almost buried in the bank and then stepped on the accelerator as hard as I could. The car shot forward into the mud so fast that a fine red spray covered the windscreen, giving it a bloodshot appearance. But I made it. And as I drew nearer the cottage I observed with relief that there was a sort of inlet to one side – drive would have been far too grand a word – leading to a large, serviceable shed, which I assumed was the garage. I pulled in, rummaged in my pocket for the bunch of keys Bob had given me and riffled through the dog-eared labels for the one marked 'Garage'. Before getting out to open the double doors I took a look at the outside of the cottage. Disappointingly, it wasn't picturesque, but that might, I told myself, be in its favour – gnarled beams and golden thatch, especially when associated with Bob Tyrrell, could well mean no running water and a ditch at the bottom of the garden. As it was, Rook's Cottage seemed the kind of place to have 'all the usual offices'. It had the air of a sensible council house: grey slate roof, cream pebble-dash walls, brown woodwork and a neat, dull garden in front bisected by a paved path leading from iron gate to front door. Through the now fading drizzle I could make out more garden at the back.

Somewhat encouraged, partly by the appearance of the cottage and partly by my victory over its very own slough of despond, I got out and dragged open the rickety wooden doors of the garage. I drove the Morris in and noticed that there was another door in the side of the shed. This opened, as I'd hoped, on to a tiny covered way leading to the back door. I closed up the front of the garage, picked up my case and a few of the loose things from the back seat, and let myself in to what would be my home for the next few months.

It's always an uphill struggle making one's mark on a new place. Every drawer knob and cupboard handle seemed to resist my enquiring hand; doorways shrank to make me stoop, high shelves receded still further as I reached up. I felt an invader in Tyrrell's cottage. It was very neat and clean, frighteningly so. The kitchen was modern, fully fitted and gleaming. The rest of the house was furnished, sparsely but adequately in an unimaginative G-plan style, and I could imagine Tyrrell walking into a furniture shop and ordering a whole set of the stuff in about five minutes flat to avoid overtaxing his imagination. The soft furnishings were of the stretchy, easily washable, don't-show-the-dirt variety and identical thin beige candlewick spreads lay over all the beds like dust sheets.

Yet despite the cottage's being in good order, no sense of tranquillity comforted me. Instead of a delightful refuge it felt like a prison. I paced about, unloading books, stuffing clothes into drawers, investigating kitchen cupboards, keeping my mounting feeling of unease at bay. I discovered, but without much cheer, that someone had been anxious for my welfare, for the electricity and water heater had been switched on and there were groceries in the fridge and cupboards.

At about seven thirty I sat down in the kitchen and opened one of the cans of ale I had found. A wave of desolation swept over me now that the protection of busyness was gone. What in hell's name was I doing here? The shiny, spotless surfaces dared me to make a mess. Outside in the bleak little garden the rain had given way to a flat, grey, saturated twilight. I tried to analyse my gloom. Urban creature that I was I had somehow pictured a quaint timbered affair with perhaps a climbing rose and hollyhocks, and inside a log fire burning between twinkling brasses. Well, I suppose that had always been unlikely – if it had been that sort of place Bob would have been letting it to Americans for vast sums. At least it was quiet – quiet and peaceful. And yet even that wasn't altogether satisfactory, for it was *too* damn quiet. Where were those reassuring rural sounds – the lowing of cows, the twittering of birds, the wind in the trees? There was just this dull, moist stillness, broken only by the starting-up of the fridge motor.

With depression settling on me like a pall and determined not to be totally enervated by it, I polished off the last of the ale, switched on the light and began to open tins for my supper. As I stood at the stove I heard a brisk knocking at the window. I peered, squinting, for the light in here made it seem quite dark outside. I could discern nothing; I went to the back door and as I opened it my visitor came round the corner, emitting a brisk, penetrating verbal salvo.

'Oh, you must be Mr Bowater, nice to meet you, I'm Dot Payne, I keep an eye on the place when Mr Tyrrell isn't here. Have you found everything alright? Mind if I pop in for a moment?' The final question appeared to be rhetorical for she was already hurrying past me into the kitchen.

With my 'Please do' frozen on my lips I turned to see a thin, bright-eyed woman with viciously permed hair and a pursed mouth. She got in her next remark before I'd had a chance to draw breath.

'I meant to leave this for you –' she thrust a note at me – 'but we had such a rush in the shop I didn't get up here in time. It's just to say where I'd put the groceries and which bed I'd made up and so on, but it doesn't matter now of course.' She withdrew the note and scrumpled it up, glanced accusingly at the baked beans bubbling fiercely on the stove and moved the saucepan.

'Thank you so much, Mrs Payne,' I said, anxious not to appear troublesome over the matter of the note. 'I was just wondering who'd been kind enough to get things ready.'

'Oh, that's no trouble. Mr Tyrrell wrote to say you hadn't been well, to make sure you were comfortable.' She shot me a piercing look. 'I'll be in a couple of mornings a week to clean round and do any bits and pieces you want.'

'That will be marvellous, but I don't suppose I'll be needing much. And don't feel you must come round two mornings a week – perhaps I could just let you know when I need a bit of sorting out?' I tried to sound as agreeable as possible.

'You've got to be looked after,' was the intractable response, a strange mixture of martyrdom and triumph. Damn Tyrrell and his tactless, officious good nature! The woman obviously regarded me as an invalid. Her orders were to look after me, and look after me she would, no matter what the personal inclinations of either of us. I'd be lucky to get any peace at all by the look of her.

'What do I owe you for all the things you bought?' I enquired, guilty about my churlish thoughts.

'Oh, Mr Tyrrell paid for those – he always puts a stock in at first. Anything you buy after you pay for. I'll do a bit of shopping for you on Thursdays if you give me a list. We close at the shop midday on Thursday.'

'The shop?'

'We run a newsagent in the village.' The fact obviously afforded her some pride for she settled her shoulders in a little gesture of self-satisfaction.

I hastened to capitalise on this moment of goodwill. 'Good heavens, in that case I wouldn't dream of imposing on your precious spare time.'

She had to concede that one. She began looking about her with quick, sharp movements of her head, like a bird.

'So.' She looked back at me. 'You've found everything.'

'Yes, thank you. I shall be very comfortable. I think I'll have something to eat and then catch an early night.' She ignored the hint. 'Oh yes, it's a nice enough little place.' She paused. 'Down for a holiday, are you?' Even as she asked, she was nodding to herself, certain I was recovering from some dreadful disease. I took great relish in correcting her.

'No, I'm down to do some work.'

'Well, I never . . . you work with Mr Tyrrell at this college, don't you?'

'Yes.'

'That's nice.'

I could just picture Bob shooting a line about academic life to Mrs Payne. She probably imagined that we spent our time smoking cigars in book-lined rooms, drinking fine old port and strolling on smooth green lawns in gowns and mortarboards. Fat chance.

'It must be an interesting life – at the university,' she said.

'It is sometimes. But it's mostly pretty routine stuff, you know, just like any other job.'

'Yes, I suppose so.' She looked at me with undisguised disappointment. What a let-down I must appear.

'Well!' I smiled genially and brought my hands together into a prayerful clap like a headmaster ending a speech. 'Thank you again, Mrs Payne, for all you've done, and I'll see you when you come next. Oh – what happens if I'm out?'

'I have a key – that is if you don't mind me letting myself in.'

'Not at all.'

'And if you want to know anything about anything you only have to ask – I know most people around here.'

'Marvellous.' I bet she did, the harpy.

'Bye-bye then.'

9

'Good-bye, Mrs Payne.'

I saw her out of the back door and returned thankfully to my beans on toast. I should certainly have to keep my wits about me if I was to stay one step ahead of Dot Payne. She was one of those people whose forte is to wreck seclusion and prise out the vulnerable introvert from his shell of privacy. As I washed up my plate I toyed briefly with the idea of dispensing with her services altogether, but that might queer Bob Tyrrell's pitch and after all, he was only thinking of me. Let her hoover and polish – and keep her distance.

The phone rang. Its penetrating insistence was quite a shock in the stillness. I somehow hadn't expected anyone to ring me, even though I'd left the number with several people. I went through into the sitting room and located the phone, perched on a hideous little teak table beside a pile of old copies of *Country Life* and *Field*. It was like a dentist's waiting room.

'Hallo?' I peered at the number on the dial. 'This is Ballacombe 277510.'

'I know – it's me.'

'Bob!'

'How are you doing down there, got everything you want?'

'Yes, thanks – you've been to a lot of trouble.'

'Not at all, not at all; no more than I'd do for any other guest. Have you met my daily woman yet? I specifically told her to cherish you.'

'Yes, I've met her. Only just got rid of her as a matter of fact.'

'You sound dubious.'

'It's just that she's – how shall I put it – enthusiastic. And since you told her I hadn't been well—'

'Which is perfectly true.'

'In a sense – but now she thinks I'm a terminal case, I'm afraid she'll never get out of my hair.'

Tyrrell guffawed. 'Old Dot's OK. She'll get the message sooner or later, and she does know all about the village.'

'She has ways of making us talk.'

Tyrrell chortled some more, then cleared his throat and said: 'I went to see Elise this afternoon.'

'Oh, how was she?' There was a short pause, he was waiting for me to go further, but I was not to be drawn.

'Browned off, what do you think?'

'If it's any consolation to her – or you – so am I at the moment.'

'It was your choice, Mike.'

'And I don't regret it. It's just adjusting to all this soggy rural solitude. It's been raining like hell down here.'

'It'll look a lot better in the morning. I shouldn't bother about work for a few days – get out, walk around, see the area. It's rather fine, in a domestic sort of way. Sitting around the house with your nose in a book won't soothe your troubled spirit. You can do that in Hampstead.'

'Don't worry, I'll get out. In fact I've made one acquaintance already. I met the vicar en route, chap called Thorne. He was able to decipher your map for me.'

Tyrrell ignored the tease. 'Yes, he's a nice enough bloke. Runs off at the mouth a bit for a man of the cloth. I can't say I've exactly joined his flock but I have been drinking with him and his missus once or twice.'

'He asked me in. I didn't like to stop, but I thought it was hospitable of him.'

'Do you want any more names? I know one or two others you might like to get in touch with.'

'Don't bother, I don't anticipate much socialising, and if you give me names I'll feel duty-bound to seek them out.'

'OK, but for Christ's sake don't mooch about on your tod sinking further and further into morbid imaginings.'

'Mooching about on my tod, as you put it, is what I came for, but I'll try and avoid the other bit.'

'And Mike –'

'Yes?'

'You might get in touch with Elise.'

'Of course I bloody will!' He'd finally riled me. Every time, I swore he wouldn't and every time he got me in the end. 'She's my wife, remember?'

'Sorry, sorry. I beg your pardon.'

I gritted my teeth. 'You're a good friend, Bob, but let us take care of ourselves.'

'Sorry again.'

There was an embarrassed silence, which Bob broke with a hearty: 'OK then. I'll be in touch. Let me know if there's anything you want.'

'Thanks, Bob.'

'All the best. *Au revoir.*'

''Bye.'

I put the phone down. It was nearly nine and the room was darkening rapidly. It was very quiet. I decided to go to bed.

I locked up the back door and the garage, remembering that there were still a lot of my belongings in the car, and went up the narrow stairs to the small front bedroom which Mrs Payne had designated mine. Like the rest of the house it was pin-neat, austere and colourless, though every comfort was present. The small dormer window between starched and faded flowered curtains looked out over the tall banks bordering the cart track to rolling fields.

It was hilly country, and up to the right of Rook's Cottage the ground sloped steeply upwards for about a mile, ending in a small wood, opaquely black between land and sky in the gathering twilight. The cart track itself petered out about a quarter of the way up this rise at the entrance to a field.

Beyond the lane to the left of the cottage the fields gave way to uncultivated heath dotted with clumps of gorse and Scotch firs. Way down on the left in the valley below the

12

heath I could make out the stubby tower of Ballacombe Church. A landmark and, even to this dispossessed agnostic, a comfort.

A couple of cars whooshed by on the wet road, their headlights flooding and fading, and a third drew up and disgorged its noisy occupants at, I believed, the entrance to the Lamb and Flag. More comfort – this time to my starved urban sensibilities.

I washed, got into bed and turned the light out at once. But instead of sleeping I leaned back wide-eyed and thought back over the events that had brought me here.

Two

It was always obvious that people regarded Elise and myself as a successful couple; both in our work and in our relationship with each other. And they were right insofar as any onlooker can be right who sees through a glass darkly. Only we two – Elise and I – knew the true paucity of our success, could feel the cold wind blowing through the cracks and see the darkness outside. Sometimes I felt that while everyone else saw us as lions, regal and confident, striding out fearless and free, lords of all we surveyed, we were like two foxes in a hole, huddling together for warmth and protection.

It was indicative of our real timidity that we never admitted this to each other. So well did we hedge ourselves about with our image that it cast its long shadow between us. We were at our best in company, when we closed ranks and did our double act with all its infinite subtleties and variations, succeeding in convincing even ourselves of what merry, well-balanced folk we were. But there was always a moment, when the guests had gone, when our party faces slipped for a moment, when we found ourselves with nothing to say, and with no sensations other than slight guilt. At these moments I often came close to saying: 'Let's admit it! Let's admit we're a sham. Wouldn't it be a relief to tell each other how craven and small-minded and ordinary we are?' But I never did. And in the end we would adjust our faces, laugh over the people we'd just seen, wash up

14

and go to bed, there – sometimes – to make tame love, and then drift apart into the relief of sleep.

It wasn't that there was any dark secret: no hideously grinning skeleton waiting to fall with a clatter from our marital cupboard. It was just that we were not and had never been what we seemed. We weren't brilliant; we were tarnished. We weren't secure; we were riddled with doubt, and the marriage itself, though destined to last, did so not because it was without flaws, but because we refused to accept their existence. The flaws in themselves did not matter – what did was our inability to confront them and, worse, our perpetual pretence that we were in some way first in life's race.

It may have been the attitudes of others towards us that started us on weaving the tangled web. Our friends seemed determined from the outset to make something of everything we did, and it was all too easy to play along with them. Even the manner of our meeting became, in retrospective conversation, a kind of Antony and Cleopatra *grand amour*, an immediate passion so powerful that nothing and nobody could say us nay. Whereas in fact I had shamelessly pinched Elise from Bob Tyrrell because I fancied her. She was as bad, abandoning him for me at a party to which he had brought her. Passion – or the semblance of it, and none of it grand – had only briefly been part of the equation. Poor Bob, he had actually become a sort of spear-carrier in our play, with his line of 'What could I do? They were so obviously crazy about each other.' It both amused people and warmed their hearts to witness such loyal and selfless friendship, to observe that we were all still friends and able to discuss it. His line would have been more correct had it read: 'What could I do? They were two of a kind, escaped from this bloody boring party when I wasn't looking . . .'

In spite of all this I should not detract from Elise's

immense desirability. When we had met four years ago I had been thirty-two and she a couple of years older – mature, cultivated, elegant. To me, accustomed to being surrounded by youthful and on the whole unkempt students, she was as intoxicating as champagne after small beer. She was the only daughter of a French mother and English father and at the time taught her mother tongue at an extremely expensive private crammer in Golders Green. But apart from her enchanting accent and Gallic elegance she was totally anglicised. In the unlikely setting of a college cocktail party, she glittered. Her only association with the place at that time was a rather one-sided liaison (his) with my bluff, good-hearted, heavy-handed friend Bob Tyrrell.

I had turned up at the party early, and on sufferance, knowing I would be bored, and anxious to do my bit and go. The Principal's sitting room, into which we were packed like sardines, was appallingly hot, and the drinks small and warm, so that even the thought of the arctic January night outside was attractive. I stood with my back pressed against bookshelves and my front against the well-upholstered bosom of Madeleine Barker, the Principal's secretary, a motherly soul now far gone in sherry and beginning to confide in me. If there is one thing guaranteed to bring on claustrophobia in the single male, it's a woman who reminds him of his auntie threatening to spill the sexual beans. I felt hot, trapped and embarrassed, and was just about to mutter my excuses and shuffle sideways in the direction of the door when a voice called my name above the hubbub and I spotted Tyrrell, stretching and waving like a drowning man over the bobbing sea of heads.

'Well, I never,' I said to Miss Barker, with the jocularity of acute relief, 'there's old Bob Tyrrell. I must go and have a word if you'll excuse me,' and without bestowing so much as another glance on her eager pink face I fought my way ungallantly from her side.

Bob Tyrrell and I squeezed and sidestepped our way through the crush and finally met like a couple of sweat-stained explorers in a clearing appropriately near the drinks table.

'Splendid,' cried Tyrrell. 'Thank God someone civilised is here. Who the hell did you find to talk to before we arrived?'

'Madeleine Barker was telling all.'

'Christ! Old dear unburdening herself, was she? Ha!' He let out a great shout of mirth. 'What a terrible experience for a young lad like you. But we're going to change all that, aren't we?' And with a flourish like a conjurer's assistant he presented his companion.

She was like a hot-house orchid: glossy, scented, perfect; a lovely natural form exquisitely improved upon.

Her skin was creamy and lustrous; her hair a silver, metallic blond, pulled tightly back into a smooth swathe at the nape of her neck; her eyes were grey, frosty but sparkling; and her mouth, though it had a somewhat firm set above a neat, pointed chin, was now curved in a closed, cat-like, delightfully secretive smile that seemed meant only for me.

'This,' said Tyrrell, 'is Elise Phillips.'

As I shook her hand and muttered something about being delighted, I thought how inexplicable it was that until this moment I had tended to favour naturalness, 'A sweet disorder in the dress' – that sort of thing. I had always found smartness unnerving and hard, but this woman carried elegance to its sublime heights and made it not a façade but an end in itself. Her soft cream wool trouser suit with its studied simplicity, her narrow gold watch, even her boots of fine wrinkled leather made every other woman in the room look dowdy.

Her handshake was surprisingly firm and brisk and while Tyrrell made introducing noises she kept her eyes on me as though connecting the information with the man before her. I learned later that this was evidence of something parasitic in her character. She drank in details about other people voraciously, never forgetting a face or a name, retaining even the most trivial details so that they would be charmed by her again and again. But of herself she gave very little. I now believe it was a defence, a kind of pre-empting of any imagined attacks or criticism. But I did not know this then, and was flattered by her smiling, fascinated gaze.

At my request she asked for a gin and tonic, and when I turned back from the bar to pass it to her Tyrrell had vanished.

'My beau,' she said, without rancour, but with just enough mischief to make the point, 'appears to have deserted me.'

'I can't imagine why,' I said.

'Thank you. What a nice compliment.' It was one of those '*coups de conversation*' at which she was a past master: a totally straightforward, almost ingenuous remark, its effect calculated to disarm.

'Who's the competition?' I asked, and with a look she indicated Tyrrell bellowing and gesturing at a grey little fellow whom I recognised as Donleavy, our man in semantics. In that look I read her complete disdain for my unfortunate friend and also, Judas that I was, the go-ahead for myself. When she turned back to me her gaze was direct, smiling and pleasant: she was waiting for me to make a move.

I decided to start with the obvious. 'You don't work here, do you?' I enquired. 'I'm sure I should have recognised you.'

'No. I do teach, but not in this rarefied atmosphere.'

'Oh? Where then?'

'I teach French to the daughters of the very rich at Hampton House.'

'Yes, I've heard of it. It's what is vulgarly known as a crammer, that right?'

'Not only vulgarly, but aptly. Cramming is exactly what we do to the young ladies and I must say it's quite frightening what good results we get from it.'

'You mean you'd prefer to say the method was a failure?'

'Quite frankly, if it wasn't my job, yes. I should like to think that the best, and therefore the most successful, form of teaching was that which drew the desire to learn from each individual, which stimulated interest first, and the assimilation of information as a natural offshoot of that interest. But, alas, there they all are at Hampton House, the spoiled darlings of the stockbroker belt, being stuffed with facts like force-fed geese, and lo and behold, at the end of it they all get their little clutch of certificates.'

'Ah well,' I said a touch pompously, 'you can blame the system for that. While we continue to have a rigid exam structure with miserably narrow syllabuses you can expect to produce a fair proportion of automaton-like exam passers.'

'Sadly,' she conceded.

'Why do you do it if it goes against the grain?'

'I suppose,' she confided with a wicked smile, 'because it doesn't irk me enough to forgo the salary. I suffer these moral and ethical pangs in considerable comfort, you know.'

She was quite delightful. 'It's people like you who ensure that bad things aren't changed,' I said reprovingly, but with a besotted smile spreading foolishly across my face. 'An intelligent woman who holds your opinions should be exerting her influence for good instead of . . . whatever sybaritic leisure pastimes you get up to in NW3.'

19

'Hardly sybaritic!' she laughed. 'I just happen to like attractive, civilised people about me, to eat good food and drink fine wine, to work in a beautiful place, to take home plenty of money and have enough time to enjoy it. There! I've put my head on the block.'

She took a sip of her gin and tonic, her eyes looking at me over the rim of the glass like a charming naughty child but without coyness. I could feel the foolish grin settling into place, marking me out as a captive. We talked on, exchanging preliminaries, sounding out each other's views in a light-hearted fashion, sizing each other up. Holding a conversation with her was as easy and satisfying as driving a Rolls. In a strange way, despite the devastating effect she had on me, her conversation was quite mannish. She never retired behind a smokescreen of affected reserve; she was not prone to those sudden fluctuations from the general to the personal which can, in many women, be so unnerving; she was frank without being shrill or strident. After about twenty minutes it was I who began to steer the conversation nearer home.

'Have you known Bob long?' I asked.

She shook her head. 'I met him at a dinner party given by mutual friends in Hampstead. Since then he's been good enough to take me to the theatre a couple of times, and to ask me along this evening.'

'Wise man. He knows this kind of do needs enlivening.'

'And yet he doesn't stay to be enlivened!'

'Ah well, that's Bob for you, all over. I wouldn't have expected him to be the most attentive of escorts.' And then, not wanting to sound disloyal, I added: 'He's an astonishingly good-hearted chap, but no social butterfly. Rather refreshing in a way.'

'In a way, yes.' For the first time I detected the merest note of feminine pique, which provoked a treacherous delight.

'. . . I'm intrigued by university life,' she was saying.

'It's not exactly Oxbridge here.'

'What does that mean?'

'It means there are no dreaming spires, no punts on rivers, no gracious leafy walks. No gilded youth, let alone fine minds.'

'But I think this university has a vitality all its own.'

'That's just London. Any big city, and especially a metropolis, is bound to be dynamic. But if anything, it saps vitality from a place like this – it's too dispersed, it never has a chance to find its identity.'

Suddenly I could hear myself becoming tendentious, grinding axes: in danger of being a bore. I stopped abruptly and asked: 'I don't suppose you'd like to look around, would you? I mean Bob seems pretty occupied.' I glanced over my shoulder at my friend, who had receded further into the crush, but whose large hands I could see flailing the air in illustration of some point or other.

Elise touched me lightly on the arm.

'I should like to,' she said, 'but let me just go and tell Bob.'

I was glad in a way that she hadn't accepted my invitation without demur. It was somehow in keeping that she should be unfailingly polite, that she wouldn't consider simply walking out on the man who'd brought her. Or that's what I thought at the time.

I drained my glass and watched her approach Bob. As she spoke to him she touched his lapel lightly, giving it a little brush, an almost wifely gesture. He looked at her, nodding, said something in reply and then something to Donleavy accompanied by a great blast of mirth from Bob himself, but barely a flicker from his audience. While he was still chortling, head thrown back, she left his side and returned to me.

'It's quite alright,' she said. 'Shall we go?'

21

We went. She went to the SCR cloakroom where she had left her coat and emerged swathed in a luxurious fox fur reaching to her ankles.

'That is the most glorious coat,' I said.

'Isn't it? It was a present, actually. I'm against real furs and would never buy one for myself. I suppose that's why I can't force myself to sell this one.'

'It looks quite fabulous.'

She bowed her head, smiling, in a pretty gesture of acknowledgement, and we walked on in silence. The corridors of the main building were echoing and empty, the students all out or in their rooms, the administrative staff having gone home. I took Elise to the library, the chapel, the huge lecture rooms, the refectory with its long trestles and hundreds of chairs still at odd angles following the after-supper scramble. Our footsteps rang out as we walked from place to place in the semi-lit emptiness. Elise looked and nodded, seemed wholly absorbed. She thrust her hands deep into the pockets of her coat: her neck and head, with its silvery cap of hair, looked very fragile rising from the great sweep of chestnut fur.

We went out of a side door and across the dark, frozen croquet lawn to where you could look out over London. The peculiar orange glow generated by a million electric lights drained the colour from our clothes and faces so, we looked ghostly.

When we turned back, driven by the biting cold, we had a clear view of the party through the brightly lit, uncurtained window of the Principal's study. Quite suddenly and unexpectedly she turned to me and said: 'I'm ravenous. Have you eaten?'

'Well – no, I haven't, but—'

'Then shall we?'

'What about Bob?' But she was already a few paces ahead of me and did not hear, or did not want to. She turned her huge collar up as if to shut out my question.

Guilty but gratified, I followed.

I took her to supper at an Italian restaurant on the Finchley Road. The place was full of students, the food pricey and indifferent and the service of the thump-and-shrug variety. But she appeared not to notice its deficiencies and cleared her plate of its ponderous burden with every evidence of relish. We did not mention Bob again. In fact, by some unspoken mutual pact, our conversation remained general.

At the end of the meal she said she'd take a cab rather than walk back to college and collect my friend, so we paused briefly in the black wind and traffic noise, waiting for one to come along. Quite easily and naturally she slipped her arm through mine and snuggled against me as though to keep warm. I kissed her, sure I was the easiest conquest she'd ever made, sure she would despise me. If she did, she didn't show it, and when I'd put her in her cab I marched back to my rooms at a terrific rate, my breath smoking like a steam engine in icy air. I never even thought of Bob Tyrrell.

From that evening the affair proceeded as though ordained by fate. With every advance in our relationship I was sure it would end there, that my luck couldn't hold, that she would surely find a man more handsome, more worldly, more brilliant than I, but to my amazement she seemed perfectly content. Perhaps the basic flaw in our marriage was that we never achieved empathy; that I looked on her from the start as a gorgeous, but alien creature, whom I was fortunate enough to have ensnared. And when, with the passage of time, those 'spots of commonness' began to stain her flawless image, there was no comforting bedrock of togetherness to fall back on.

I asked Elise to marry me at the beginning of April, and

she accepted. At our register office wedding in May Bob Tyrrell was chief witness (Elise's idea), with his upper lip ramrod-stiff and his affable grin petrified on his face. Elise was sweet with him, and though I watched anxiously for signs of brooding jealousy, he seemed anaesthetised by shock.

We were well off, despite Elise giving up work, for her elderly parents gave us a substantial sum as though we were a couple of starry-eyed kids in our twenties, both of us had a bit of capital and I was earning a comfortable salary. We bought a tall, spacious Edwardian house near the Heath, which Elise had decorated in calm good taste, and which easily accommodated our many books, pictures and plants. We acquired a nearly new Mercedes with the proceeds from Elise's Mini Cooper, but retained my ancient, gleaming Morris as a run-around. The college was Elise's oyster – both my colleagues and my students adored her, and she revelled in it. It was gratifying to be regarded as the man with everything: so gratifying indeed that it prevented me from studying my situation too closely.

After about eighteen months reality began to set in. I'd call it the rot, but it wasn't as obvious as that. It was more as though a fine veil that had hung between us had been drawn back so that for the first time we confronted each other without the soothing illusions of soft-focus. God knows, we tried to preserve our ignorant bliss, and I believe to this day that Elise succeeded. For she lived through the eyes of other people – if they thought her beautiful, intelligent, charming, that was enough for her. Why look deeper? She regarded any means to this end as acceptable. For a woman so clever and so cultured, she was profoundly concerned with appearance, especially her own. Not with the trivial detail – you never caught her patting her hair or dabbing at her nose with a powder puff – but with the dedicated nurturing of face and body through diet, exercise and various rites of skin and hair. I never saw her with curlers in, or cream on her face – she would have thought it shameful to parade the mechanics of self-maintenance. No matter how exhausted we both were, she would always retire to the bathroom to do God knew what with herself, to emerge glowing and exquisite, well-groomed even in her natural state when all grooming had apparently been purged. She would change, cleverly, from sophisticate to ingénue, her hair silky and curtain-straight, her cheeks rosy, the soft hollows of her body fragrant with the innocent, wicked scent of baby lotion.

To begin with, my delight at this vision of loveliness knew no bounds. It was exciting, gratifying, enchanting. Other men's wives, I felt smugly sure, in order to maintain elegance in the daylight hours had to affright their husbands with Kirby-grips and face-masks. This illusion was only reinforced by memories of women I'd slept with who had come to bed in full war-paint, hoping to kid themselves and me.

But my fool's paradise didn't last. The simple fact was, Elise didn't love me. Nor – I can say it now – did I love her. Not really. I was infatuated, and she was used to that and knew how to play me along without the least emotional investment. I know now that she was not a bad person; she meant me no harm, she was simply doing what she was best at out of a curious, preprogrammed politeness. She had beauty, brains, charm and social graces in abundance – but she lacked passion.

For a while I worshipped her, but it was an image I worshipped, not a flesh and blood woman.

The hollowness of our marriage began to take its toll. I felt suffocated; caught in a trap of my own making whose very soft and yielding quality made it as escape-proof as quicksand. As in a dream, I suffered the agony of not being able to communicate my feelings, or if I did, of not being understood. I was surrounded by smiling, jocular people clapping me on the back but when I tried to speak, to explain to them how things really were, my lips twisted into an acquiescent grin, and no sound came out.

When we'd been married about two years I began to suffer from depressions. Nothing seemed to go well for me, and I felt not the smallest enthusiasm for anything. I was so mentally exhausted that the mere business of getting through the day was an effort. These episodes wore off, of course, and when each had passed I found it hard to remember its blackness. But over a period of a year or so they became more frequent and acute. When I was depressed I experienced the sensation of other people drifting away from me: it was as though the unreality of my relationship with Elise was keeping me in a suspended state of non-communication with everyone.

And then, as I went from bad to worse, I was plunged into crisis by a shocking series of events at college.

At the beginning of the academic year, the usual batch of freshers had arrived in the English department, all enthusiasm, innocence and zits, ripe for the disenchantment of university life. There were fewer than usual that year but the standard was high and one boy in particular, a scholar from Winchester named James Yates, showed exceptional brilliance. He had a resonant, middle-class voice, a pink and white complexion and a thatch of brown hair which grew longer and more unkempt as fashion dictated. He was in my tutorial group and the fact that he, like myself, was from public school but was apparently unscathed by that odd experience, gave us common ground. I found James likeable and sympathetic as well as clever. Like many clever people he was lazy, but neither vain nor arrogant. He had simply never been stretched and therefore felt that he was safe. I felt I should indicate to him that this was not necessarily the case, and that he would quite simply not get his degree if he persisted in doing only what pleased him. The result of this homily was that he continued to neglect the areas of the course which bored him but raced even further ahead in those he favoured.

Owing to a shortage of hall accommodation Elise and I were asked to take a couple of students – a different pair each term – to live in our house, and this was when James really entered our lives, for he and an Indian lad named Sanjay were allocated to us for the spring session. It was a bad time for me but the presence of these two, and of James in particular, cheered me.

They ate in college but would return in the evening, when they'd nothing better to do, to work in their rooms. As often as not they'd emerge at intervals to make coffee and we'd get talking, sometimes for hours, with Elise in her element as patron, hostess and attractively unobtainable older woman. James made no bones about his feelings for her. His eyes rested on her adoringly and he was full of praise. He soon endeared himself to her and I, like a fool, found the whole thing rather touching, not to say flattering. I was interested in his opinion, as one of the new honest generation with their different set of values: if James, from his vastly different perspective, found my wife desirable, then I must have been right all along. Quite sure that the situation was well under Elise's iron control I positively encouraged it. And indeed she did seem to strike the right note, charming but slightly maternal.

'You know,' observed James one evening, 'I'd like to think I was non-materialistic but seeing you two with all this, I'm not sure I could settle for anything less.'

'You may have to. Your generation has a hard row to hoe.'

'But I thought we were the affluent ones – more money than sense, I thought that was the line.'

Elise laughed and shrugged pleasantly, not admitting

defeat, but loth to become involved in a real argument. I took him up, since I had understood perfectly what she meant.

'You may live in an affluent society, but also a harder, more competitive one which prefers speed and efficiency to quality and care, and dishes out its rewards accordingly. Your riches will be hard won and hard to hang on to – I'm glad I'm not in your well-heeled shoes.'

He listened to me, but kept his eyes, smilingly, on Elise's face. 'Of course, it's me who wants to be in yours. You're corrupting me.' He gave this ungrammatical pronouncement a multiplicity of meanings, leaning forward and gazing into my wife's eyes, his head slightly to one side. The question was plain to read. I chose to ignore his cheek partly because it was so open, and partly because I liked and admired James and chose to take it as a compliment that he fancied my wife and was not ashamed to say so. I felt proud of Elise's fidelity, though in my heart I knew it to be a case of *faute de mieux*, and her composure gave me a false sense of security.

James now kneeled on the floor in front of her, like some suppliant squire at the court of chivalrous love. We laughed, but he was only half joking.

'Look at you. You're perfect. There isn't a student in the place who doesn't adore you. How could I make do with less?' Still receiving no encouragement from Elise, beyond a polite smile, he turned and addressed me: 'I ask you, how could I?'

'That's different.' I was going to be rational, at all costs. 'There are plenty of lovely girls around for a young blade like yourself.'

'Don't refer to me as though I were a commodity, you two,' said Elise.

'But you are a commodity!' James spun back towards her as though the mere sound of her voice fanned his ardour to new heights. 'The most precious there is, like a superb jewel, the only one of its kind, that everyone wants just for the thrill of saying it's theirs.'

'You have the oddest line in compliments for a boy of your age,' said Elise with her tenderest, remotest smile, and I blessed her for her unfaltering *savoir-faire*. Now she rose, murmuring something about making more coffee, and gracefully terminating the conversation, causing discomfort (as I thought) to no one.

And yet I was tricked at every turn by them. Like a trusting child – a doting idiot – I watched them play out their little charade under my very nose. In my home, in front of my television, at my dinner table. I observed James's devotion, but in my patronising early middle age I imagined him to be still shallow and readily discouraged. When I found out that he was neither, and that, what was more, no discouragement had been given, it was already too late.

The discovery was presaged by a horrible experience. It happened one night when I was returning late from a departmental meeting. To get back to the side road where I'd parked the Merc I had to walk across the forecourt of the new science block, opened with much unnecessary expense and unwieldy ceremony by a junior minister a couple of years back. It was an elegant, modern building, containing some of the largest and best-equipped lecture rooms in the college. Now it was mainly in darkness, except for a couple of lights in one of the labs on the first floor. The lofty, spacious entrance hall, in daylight resembling that of a smart American hotel, was a great black cave behind wide glass doors that reflected the shadows of the street. As I came level with these doors I glanced in with the idle curiosity which prompts one to look into other people's front rooms. I looked, passed on and then, realising what I had seen, walked back and this time peered more closely.

As I looked my stomach heaved and my head began to buzz, I thought I would faint, but something, sheer lunatic curiosity, compelled me forward. I pushed open the glass door and ran over to the lift. The darkness, thickened by my own nausea, made it hard to see, but I felt something sticky on the soles of my shoes, I put my hand down and it came away dark and damp. Frantically I pulled at the lift door but it seemed to be jammed, and I shouted, I don't know what, a bellow of sheer terror.

'Mr Bowater?' Brilliant light flooded the hallway and the college porter, Dawson, appeared from the street, his torch in his hand, a look of consternation on his face. I screamed at him: 'There's blood coming from the lift, look! Help me, for Christ's sake!'

'Sorry, sir?'

'Blood, seeping under . . . I saw . . .' I looked down at the floor where Dawson's puzzled gaze rested. 'It was there . . .' I said.

But there was nothing there. The floor glinted with a bright, clinical cleanliness. I looked at my hands. They were clean. My shoes were dry. Gradually the sickness left me, but I was weak as a kitten. Dawson, giving me a side-long look, came over and pressed the lift button, and at once the little mocking, tracking light came down the numbers from six to one – the lift had been on the top floor.

'The lift was up top sir,' said Dawson. 'There's a couple of lab assistants up there, I gave them the key.'

'Yes, I'm sorry.'

'Are you alright, sir? You don't look well.'

'No, I wasn't for a moment, Dawson. I felt extremely ill – I'm afraid that was the trouble.'

'You'd better get on home, sir. Like me to call you a minicab?'

'No, I've got the car. I'll be alright in a minute.'

He looked at me disbelievingly and then, with an almost imperceptible shrug, left the building. I remained, staring down at the glossy expanse across which that slick of blood had crept. As if to underline my foolishness the lift light began to track upwards again, summoned by the departing lab assistants.

Nauseous and shivering I hurried to the car. Already the incident seemed unreal, a dream, and yet the mere memory of those feelings is still enough to make me shudder. When I got home I didn't mention it to Elise, who was already half asleep, and the boys were out at some late party or other, so I went to bed, my teeth chattering like a sick child, scared to close my eyes because of the horrors in my head.

In the next few days the household seemed to mirror my own depression. Sanjay remained closeted in his room, studying, James was uncharacteristically taciturn and morose and Elise brittle. It was as though we moved around the flat each encased in our own fragile protective shell, which the least touch might shatter.

Then on Friday night, when James was out at a film society meeting, and Sanjay gone to friends for the weekend, Elise said: 'I don't know whether you've noticed, Michael, but James is very persistent.'

'Persistent?'

'In his attentions. To me.'

Her solemnity was almost droll. I looked up from the essays I was marking, ready to tease her, but her expression dared me to mock. She was in deadly earnest.

'I'm sorry darling,' I said, putting down my pen. 'Is it getting to be a bore?'

'It's getting to be far more than that. He wants to sleep with me.'

'I'm sure he does.'

'He is extremely persuasive.' Suddenly her eyes met

mine directly, and she stiffened slightly as though she had just reached a decision. 'This afternoon he succeeded.'

'Go on.' I felt nothing – a mini-death.

'When I got back from town he was writing in his room. There we were, alone in the flat. He was talking as he usually does. He kissed me—'

'It takes two to kiss.'

'It seemed perfectly innocuous, I could see no reason to object.'

Unfortunately, I could believe that. Although all kinds of terrible doubts and questions were rearing their heads in my mind, I could all too clearly picture James, with his candid blue eyes and his sweet directness: hard not to trust, perhaps harder still to resist.

'And then you went to bed.'

'Yes.'

'To what effect?' I could feel something inside me curling and shrivelling to nothing, like paper in a fire, so that only the little dry grey ashes of feeling were left.

'There's no need to be so cold and remote. Aren't you angry?'

'No. How would you like me to behave? Just say, and I'll do my best. I wouldn't want to let down the production with a poor performance.'

'Don't be childish. You ask to what effect, well I'll tell you. None. It was hopeless, ridiculous, humiliating for both of us. He was very upset.'

'*Upset?*' I clasped my head with tight fingers to stop the madness growing.

'Yes, upset!' Elise had become quite shrill. She took a little jerky step towards me as if she would do something. 'Upset because it didn't work, upset because I was cruel.' Her voice dropped sharply on the last word and she withdrew again, clasping her arms around herself as though in a straitjacket. 'He cried.'

There seemed to be nothing to say. I think we both felt so ashamed, so belittled by our situation that we could not bring ourselves to look each other in the eye, let alone fight. Her humiliation, my lack of anger, our sad, tepid relationship. In the end, after a full minute of silence, all I wanted to know was: 'What the hell did you say to him?'

'I don't want to think about it. He's going away.'

'I see.'

After another agonising silence Elise moved towards the door. 'I'm going to bed.' I nodded. Then, as an afterthought, she said, 'Anyway, I think he overreacted.' And then she went.

Three

Overreaction or not, James did go. He didn't return to his room that night or the next, and his fellow-students claimed to know nothing. Out of concern and also because it was my duty, I called his home number in Gloucestershire.

'Oh, how naughty of him!' exclaimed Mrs Yates, who had one of those forever-girlish voices typical of a certain kind of upper-class Englishwoman. 'Yes, he is here, he's not feeling well. And actually he does look very peaky. We dragged him round to the doctor and I think it's just a case of being run-down. You know what they are at that age, well of course you do in your job, they burn the candle at both ends and don't feed themselves properly—'

'He's boarding with my wife and myself this term,' I pointed out, 'so rest assured he's not starving in a garret.'

'Of course, how rude that must have sounded, it's just that Emily – our eldest – had glandular fever at about this age and it was a *complete* nightmare . . .' She rattled on about Emily for a bit, which I found less annoying than I might have done because of the relief – relief that James had chosen to feign illness.

'Well,' I said when she'd finished, 'I'm glad we've cleared that up. Tell him I called, and hope he feels better soon. But you might also say that he should have let someone know what he was doing and where he was going, and also that he'll need to provide a doctor's note when he comes back.'

'Definitely. I'll make sure he gets the message, good and proper, don't you worry.'

'Thank you.'

I was about to ring off when she added: 'And Mr Bowater – can I just say that in spite of my earlier gaffe he thinks the world of you and Mrs Bowater and has mentioned you both in despatches.'

'Good. Well, I'm glad. We'll hope to have him back with us soon,' I lied.

After I'd put the phone down I reflected that of course James would not automatically assume that Elise and I discussed what had happened, rather the reverse. His attitude to me would surely be one of guilt and insecurity, of wanting to cover up and make amends. I had nothing with which to reproach myself.

One thing it showed me, and that was the transforming power of love. I was humbled by it. Even if it was puppy love, infatuation, whatever, James was in the grip of something I'd never experienced. It made me realise that what I'd felt for Elise, even in the early days, was no more than a kind of ardent acquisitiveness, a futile wish to *own* her beauty, elegance and imperturbable good taste. It's shaming to admit that I wanted to be, as the advertisements put it, the envy of my friends. The unsavoury expression 'trophy wife' hadn't been coined back then, but it exactly described the role she played in my life and emotions.

And to be fair to myself, Elise was no better. She probably thought that my slavish admiration, my status and so on would be enough. Now, she was visibly shaken by the turn of events. Try as she might to convey an impression of objectivity and worldly wisdom there was no escaping the simple fact that she had responded to James's advances, and was moved and appalled by the devastation she had caused.

It was a measure of the strangeness of our relationship, its peculiarly lifeless sophistication, that I never once even considered playing the wronged husband. My response to my wife's admission (her tone was far from confessional) was one of what I can only describe as irritation. Intense irritation, but no more than that. How could the cool, composed Elise allow herself to do something so messy? How could she threaten our carefully maintained and much-envied stability, our perfect couplehood? Underlying all these unworthy thoughts was the most unworthy one of all – that we would be rumbled. That James, who, however reprehensible his behaviour had been, was subject to real, strong feelings, would go out there and cry on someone's shoulder and possibly, human nature being what it was, distort the truth to suit his own emotional needs. He had chosen not to do so with his parents, perhaps out of some misplaced loyalty to me, but I doubted that any such scruples would prevent him from telling his friends when he got back.

It was anxiety about this, more than any desire for real rapprochement, that made me suggest to Elise that we go out for lunch *à deux* on Sunday, a couple of days after she'd confided in me. The intervening two days had been characterised by a superficial normality, but since superficiality was second nature to us, our defence and shield, it might have been worse.

Still, Elise was unusually enthusiastic about the idea.

'We could go out of town – find somewhere nice in the country.'

'The country?' I couldn't conceal my surprise. She was quintessentially urban, metropolitan even.

'Yes, why not?'

'I didn't think you liked the country.'

'Pah!' She was the only person I knew who could use this exclamation effectively. 'I don't want to live there, but it's nice to visit.'

'So as to appreciate the city more,' I suggested.

'Absolutely. And it would be a change, it would do us good.'

'Then that's what we shall do,' I said.

Driving out to the four-star coaching inn in Suffolk, which was about as much rural chic as Elise could take, she said: 'You're not angry with me?' Her tone was curious rather than anxious.

'No.'

'Why not?' The same coolly enquiring note.

'Because I don't mind.' I didn't say 'care' – that would have been too harsh. But it was still a relief. For perhaps the first time, we were being direct with each other, the terms of our marriage were being acknowledged. I hoped she saw the exchange in the same light.

'Good,' she said. Her hands, slender and pale, lay in her lap loosely linked, utterly relaxed – this was no feigned insouciance. 'You are right. It was nothing. A blunder on his part, an error of judgement on mine. I do regret upsetting the poor boy, though . . .'

'Every young man needs his heart broken once,' I said. 'Preferably by a beautiful older woman.'

It was surreal: I was congratulating her. And she, of course, accepted the compliment with practised grace.

'So I did him a favour.'

'I believe so.'

She gave her silvery laugh.

Later though, in the restaurant of the hotel, when we'd eaten well and drunk expensively – Elise was an unashamed wine snob – she couldn't resist poking the situation with a stick.

'Would it have been different,' she asked musingly, 'if I'd fallen in love with him?'

'Yes. Of course.'

'You'd have been angry with me then?'

37

We were oh, so close to acknowledging the unthinkable. But it was a case of 'you go first' and I declined the invitation.

'I'd have been sad.'

'Sad . . .' She thought about this, rolling the stem of her glass between her fingers. 'Sadness is for a *fait accompli*.'

'There would be nothing I could do. You've always been a woman who knows her own mind.'

'And you've always been a flatterer!'

With this, the weirdly flirtatious nature of the occasion was restored.

After lunch, with the sun low and the afternoon shortening before us, we went for a walk. Not a country walk – Elise wasn't wearing the shoes for that – but one around the fine old centre of the town. It was one of those places whose central core has remained unchanged, timeless: a handsome fifteenth-century church, a market square, several snug pubs, a timbered town hall, and half a dozen narrow streets with well-maintained Tudor houses, and inviting shops full of second-hand books, antiques, that sort of thing. We browsed. It was the sort of situation which made us happy. Elise was born to shop, she exuded good taste and as a result most shopkeepers were only too delighted to let her wander about on their premises whether she purchased or not, as a kind of human advertisement. When she found a place that sold the kind of sleek, silk and cashmere minimalist outfits that she liked, the lady proprietor approached her like the Second Coming, so I arranged to meet her there in half an hour and went to look at second-hand books, an activity that could always keep me happily absorbed.

Because of the position of the autumn sun, the roof tops were brightly lit, but the streets were in deep shadow. Some of the shops even had their lights on, which gave them a prematurely wintry look. About twenty yards up the road from the clothes shop I came to a corner from which a narrow side street scuttled away, lit only by the glow from the occasional window. It was charming, like something from *The Tailor of Gloucester*, and because there was no one else to be seen I had the pleasurable sense of having made a discovery.

I turned down it and as I did so the sun dipped below the chimneys so it was even darker and the little antiquarian bookshop, which I had instinctively known would be there, was all rosy and cluttered and inviting like a kind of indoor garden. An old-fashioned bell clanged its tongue as I opened the door, but as so often with these places there was no one in sight, nor did anyone hurry out from a back room to find out what I wanted. All was still, and there was an atmosphere of calm and trust, and that characteristic scent of old books, as though you could breathe in the words, the thoughts, the imaginings that crowded the place . . .

Feeling peaceful, content even, for the first time in days I browsed the shelves. Here and there were chairs, some laden with more books, or piles of old periodicals, but one was empty and inviting, so feeling like some unlikely Goldilocks that it was intended for me, I sat down to take a closer look at three randomly selected books.

The first was a wonderful old travel book from before the Great War, a time capsule as well as a description of the author's journey around the Black Sea; the second, a memoir by one of those now sadly defunct mandarin Tories, aristocratic, liberal, classically educated and morally fastidious, a dinosaur in current political terms but an immensely engaging one. I knew I'd probably buy both of them, and half a dozen more.

The third one I picked up because of its title, *Testing Time*, though in the past those words wouldn't even have caught my eye, let alone my attention. It was by someone called Spearman, with my initials, M.J. The strapline below the title on the cover said that it was 'A layman's exploration of life's story': again, that would usually have been too pat, too commercial, frankly too common for my ascetic academic taste, but just now it spoke to me. I riffled through the pages self-consciously like some innocent young husband with a top-shelf magazine. A chapter heading caught my eye: 'For each man kills the thing he loves' . . . and another, a song lyric I think: 'I knew you before, long before we met' . . . A third: 'Remembrance of things to come'.

Idly, knowing I'd buy this one too, I turned to the back flyleaf. And there I was.

I was looking at a photograph of myself, but subtly altered. Older, but not much; not heavier, but pouchier. My hair longer at the back, thinner on top. I was less neat, I wore a dark sweater, my eyes were duller. This me had an uncared-for appearance. But it was me just the same.

A shock wave shot through me like a thousand volts. My face and hands went ice-cold, my stomach swirled, there was bile in my mouth.

'Alright there?'

It was the bookseller, finally checking up on his only customer. He was young and burly, in denims and desert boots. His smile was as big as all outdoors.

'Found something that interests you?'

'Yes, thanks. Just browsing.'

'It's what we're for. Be as long as you like.' He glanced around. 'No crowd problem that I can see. I'll get back to my VAT, give a shout if you need me.'

He returned to his back room and at once the dense quiet of the shop closed behind him, cutting him off like a thick, invisible curtain.

Fearfully, with a racing heart and a dry mouth I tilted my head and glanced from the corner of my eye at the book in my hands.

Same book; same title. Same photograph. But it wasn't

me. I was as sure of that now as I'd been sure, less than a minute ago, of the opposite.

Trembling with agitation I rose, placed all three books on the chair and crept from the shop like a thief. The bell, like the giant's magic harp, rang, 'Master! Master!' but by that time I was out in the narrow street and walking fast, unsteadily, towards the main road.

In the dress shop Elise was nowhere to be seen. The lady assistant was doing something inconsequential to a row of smooth capes on hangers. She looked up, brows raised in an expression of douce, elegant disapproval as I burst in.

'Where's my wife?' I asked. I blurted it out, as though I suspected the woman of kidnapping her. She smiled and nodded towards the back of the shop.

'She's trying something on. I'll tell her you're here, she can show you.' She looked over her shoulder as she walked towards the cubicle and added: 'I think you'll like it.'

I stood there almost rocking on my heels. I was suddenly absolutely exhausted. There was a long mirror on the wall and I saw myself reflected in it – a thin, wild, disarrayed man, the sort a lady would step aside to avoid on the street.

'Michael . . . ?'

It was Elise, dressed in a smooth column of cream cashmere, bias-cut with a hint of swathing at the neck and at the hip, a style that only the impeccably slender could wear.

'That was quick,' she said. 'Did you not find anything interesting?'

'No.'

'Are you alright? You look awful.'

'I'm fine.'

She wasn't really interested. 'Do you like this? What do you think? Shall I get it?'

They were all questions addressed to herself, perhaps to

the assistant, least of all to me, but I answered simply to hear my own voice answering, to know I was present in the prosaic and comforting here and now.

'Definitely. You look lovely.'

The assistant wafted me a message of approval and gratitude. I waited outside while she paid. As we walked back to the hotel where we'd left the car I glanced down the side street and saw the bookseller, now with a heavy plaid jacket on, locking up the shop.

Elise carried a huge white carrier bag with shiny black rope handles. She was incandescent with pleasure over her purchase of the perfect dress.

'. . . always when you're not looking for it,' she was saying. 'But I thought you'd come back loaded with dusty old books! What happened? You were only gone a second.'

'Oh,' I said. 'I changed my mind.'

And thought what an odd expression that was.

When we got back, with Elise still in sparkling spirits, the house was dark except for the lamp we'd left on in the hall, and Sanjay's room, whose curtained window glowed bronze. We did that married thing of going straightaway to perform our separate, preordained tasks. Elise put her bag and carrier bag down on the hall chair and went through to the drawing room to close the curtains, turn on the lights and switch on music – it was a tape from the night before, Peter Pears singing Britten's setting of English folk songs. 'The Foggy, Foggy Dew', its stealthy lewdness made lyrical by the beauty of the singer's voice. I went first to the kitchen to put the kettle on, then upstairs to knock on Sanjay's door and confirm that we were back at the helm, so to speak.

As I crossed the hall the phone rang. I saw Elise pick up the receiver to answer it. As I reached the first floor landing I saw a figure at the foot of the next flight, the one that went up to the students' floor.

'Sanjay . . . ?'

'Michael!' It was Elise, from downstairs. 'Michael, that was James's mother . . . ?' Her voice held an upward, questioning inflection – she was checking that I could hear.

'Yes?'

'He's coming back, apparently. He left this morning.'

'Yes,' I said again. We gazed steadily at one another. 'He's here.'

Elise said 'Hallo James' and withdrew to the bedroom to hang up her new dress.

'Do you think I could have a word, Michael?' he asked.

We'd always encouraged students living with us to use our Christian names, but now I had to fight the urge to pull rank.

'Of course.'

We went downstairs to the study. On the way I enquired chattily after his health and he replied that he was fine now, thanks. Well, bully for you, I thought. It wasn't my heart that was wounded, it was my manly pride.

I closed the door of the study and invited him to sit down. 'What can I do for you?'

He sat with legs wide apart, his arms resting on his knees, fingers linked, head bowed; said, without looking up: 'I suppose you know about what happened?'

'Why don't you tell me, just in case?'

'So, you do.'

'My wife told me.'

'I'm sorry,' he mumbled, like a child being given a roasting by his father for teasing the cat.

'Not half as sorry as we are,' I snapped thinly. For some reason his fumbling apology enraged me more than the offence itself. Perhaps I needed a fight to prove something to myself.

He shook his head dazedly. 'Yup . . . yup . . . yeah, of course . . .'

I waited for a moment. I was standing – standing over him, in effect. I didn't actually drum my fingers and tap my foot, but my impatience and irritation must have been obvious. Not enough to make him look up, though.

He pushed his fingers into his hair; cleared his throat. 'I'll move out, of course.'

'No need,' I said. 'It makes no difference to us.'

'It does to me.'

'Then move out.'

Suddenly he did look up and his expression was quite different from what I'd imagined – not that of a whipped pup but of a passionate and furious young man, reddened and swollen with the strength of his feelings. The phrase 'pumped-up' took on fresh meaning.

'I am in love with her, you know.' His voice was strong now, without hesitancy or apology. The gauntlet was well and truly thrown down.

'I dare say you are. Like half the students in this place.' I wanted to kill him with casualness, to drain the heat from his little drama. To cut him down to size.

'No, nothing like that.' He dismissed my sarcasm with the clean, sharp weapon of certainty. 'Properly.'

'And how, from your vast experience of the subject would you define "properly"?'

'I want her happiness more than my own.'

Jesus God.

'Very commendable.' Even I could hear how unworthy, how bloodless, that sounded.

'So, of course I'll go somewhere else.'

I remembered, a little late, my pastoral responsibilities. 'I'll contact the accommodation office on your behalf.'

'There's no need.'

'It's my duty.'

'If that's how you see it, then it's up to you.' He stood up. In the past two minutes the balance between us had shifted completely and now I appreciated for the first time how much taller and heavier he was than me, a former school rugger player. He could easily have knocked me over. In fact when he put his hands in his pockets I construed it, probably wrongly, as a gesture of restraint, which only increased my sense of being belittled.

I went to show him out, but he didn't move. In fact he didn't even turn towards the door as I opened it but said, with his back to me: 'Would it be out of the question for me to have a word with her?'

'Absolutely.'

There was a nanosecond's silence which told me I'd hit home.

'OK.'

It was that 'OK' as if he'd agreed to a suggestion rather than taken an order, which made me want to have the last word, to inflict one more cut before he left the room. As he passed me I said very, very quietly: 'She told me what a disaster it was. Whatever the nature of your feelings for her, she had none for you other than pity. "Pathetic" was the word she used. You ought to know that.'

He paused while I spoke and then went in silence. The front door closed quickly, softly behind him. I was left standing there with the feeling that though I was in the right, had occupied by any standard the moral high ground, had exacted fully justified punishment on the wrongdoer, I had still, in some deeper way, lost.

Elise came down and paused at the foot of the stairs.

'He's gone out?'

'Yes.'

'How is he?'

'Oh . . .' I waved a dismissive hand, turned out the study light and closed the door behind me, 'you know. Wound up.

Wants to move out, which I think is right. I'll help him find somewhere.'

'Poor James,' she murmured. She came over and rested her forehead on my shoulder in a graceful, submissive gesture. 'Poor Michael.'

'I'm alright.'

She sighed tremulously. 'Silly me.'

With the scent of her hair wafting up to me, and the light pressure of her head on my shoulder I thought, Silly? Yes, perhaps that's what this all was . . . just silly.

I sat up late, staring blankly at the television and drinking whisky. I had some idea that I was waiting for James but to what purpose I didn't know. It was obvious from what Elise had said that, whatever his behaviour, he had suffered, and would suffer, enough. So what was I going to say or do? To call myself a wronged husband would be totally false since I had condoned and encouraged everything but the act itself. And yet to affect suave indifference would be hypocrisy. In the event I was spared the decision. At about midnight, the phone rang.

It was the Principal.

'Michael?'

'Principal – I was almost asleep. Thinking of calling you, actually, over a matter of—'

'Michael, this is urgent.' His voice was tight and sharp. 'I'm afraid something shocking has happened.'

All at once I was trembling, taut as a bowstring. Elise, ghostly in a long white negligée came out of the bedroom and stood there in the doorway in the twilight, listening.

'What?' I asked, though my sour mouth and cold, sticky palms anticipated the answer.

'It's that young lad in your department. James Yates – he lodges with you this session, doesn't he?'

'That's right, why—?'

46

'No point in prevaricating. He killed himself.'

I knew. I knew. I looked at Elise, who had come a few steps forward, her eyes questioning something she had read in my face. I cupped my hand over the receiver and said, baldly: 'James killed himself.' I wanted to hurt her and I succeeded. She gave a little gasp and turned away, her head bowed.

'Michael – are you there?'

'Yes.'

'I'm truly sorry it has to be so brutal, but there seems to be no other way to say these things, and God knows I'm going to have to do it often enough in the next twenty-four hours.'

'I understand. What happened?'

'He went to a film society meeting in that big lecture hall in the science block. He stayed behind afterwards, stole a dissecting instrument and cut his wrists in the lift . . .' He paused, said in a strange voice: 'The mess was appalling.'

'What a way to do it.'

'He seemed to want to shock.'

I tried to speak.

'Michael.'

'Yes. Do I have to do anything?'

'I've handled the immediate problems, but I'd like your moral support tomorrow – his parents are coming.'

'Very well.'

I rang off. Elise was crying quietly but I didn't go to her. Instead I saw the hallway dark as a cave, the tight-shut doors of the lift leaking blood like a fresh wound.

The following weeks were a nightmare. More than the grief I felt over James's suicide, or my resentment at Elise's treachery was the exquisite torture of guilt. I was sure that my own part in the chain of events had been crucial. After all, I had *known*, I had been shown, and yet I had been unable or unwilling to go further; I had not had the courage to make the leap from those things I knew by observation to those I knew or suspected from instinct, and the result of my timidity was this – this messy, wasteful tragedy.

Elise, in her coolly correct way, had told Tyrrell (in strict confidence, knowing it would leak out) that James had suffered from a feeling of inferiority to which sexual rejection had delivered the final blow. I had to admire her. It was so nearly the truth as to be acceptable to the two of us, who knew the real truth, and by putting the word about discreetly she had pre-empted further investigation. Of course there were questions to be answered, formalities to be undergone, and we went through them like automatons, habituated by experience to keeping our secret.

Bob Tyrrell, it must be said, was a tower of strength. Being a good chap was his forte, so he probably rather enjoyed the whole thing, particularly as my debilitated state made it necessary for him to minister to Elise. Or rather to keep her company, for she did not seem to require ministration. It was he who pushed and assisted me to get a sabbatical for the autumn term, he who offered his cottage and got the thing organised. He spent nearly all his time with us, clucking and fussing and making arrangements. His most valuable contribution was to obviate the need for confrontation between Elise and myself. So expert had we become at papering over cracks that we were even able to do so now, when the bricks and mortar themselves were crumbling. How delicately we trod, how careful we were only to skim the surface.

I knew very well that Elise would have no qualms about letting me go away alone, for three good reasons. Firstly and most importantly she knew I didn't want her there; secondly, she didn't want to come, least of all to stroke my fevered brow; thirdly, she needed time to lick her wounds and restore her self-respect among people who admired her.

But Tyrrell was deeply shocked.

'Alone, old boy? You're crazy.'

'Very probably.'

'No, no, I didn't mean . . .' He was embarrassed. 'What does Elise say about it?'

'She says OK.'

'I don't understand you. You two of all people, why should you want to be apart at a time like this?'

'Look, Bob, it's all been worked out. We're neither of us ourselves at the moment, you know that. I feel I must get out of town to find my feet, whereas the country's a recipe for crack-up as far as she's concerned. We've agreed to differ. Let's leave it at that.'

'There's nothing – wrong – is there?' His heavy-handed tact and stupidly solicitous expression were infuriating.

'Of course! Every bloody thing's wrong! For Christ's sake, Bob, treat us like adults and leave us alone.' Then, remembering his kindness I took a grip on myself and produced the lie he hoped to elicit. 'Nothing's wrong between us, if that's what you mean.'

'Good, good! She's quite a girl, your wife.'

'There you are then,' I said, waspishly. 'Now's your chance.'

'Don't, Mike,' he said. I don't suppose he ever forgave me.

A few weeks later I was installed in Rook's Cottage, with the dark, waiting fields outside.

Four

T he following day was one of washy, pale sunshine, the last of the clouds being chased across a pale sky by a brisk wind. I woke early – I suppose it must have been the strangeness of the surroundings – and when I'd had some tea and toast I began to look round the cottage more closely.

The house itself was actually of a fair size – the rooms were small but there were several of them – four bedrooms upstairs, and downstairs a stiff little dining room and sitting room ('parlour' was the word that sprang to mind) in addition to the well-fitted-out kitchen. All the rooms were square and plain and painted in a uniform light cream, not dingy but far from exciting. You had to hand it to Mrs Payne, she did do her job: the whole place shone – even, I noticed, the extra bedrooms and other areas not in use. Yet the cottage was not snug, not the cosy rural idyll I'd pictured at all. I would be comfortable here, have everything I wanted, be well looked after no doubt by the redoubtable Dot, but it was distinctly short of quaint charm. The same applied to the garden. It was neither bosky and romantic nor picturesquely packed with hollyhocks and delphiniums. It was neat and rather plain – mostly grass which was, I noticed, recently mowed: in the front, a narrow border of wallflowers ran along beneath the bank that edged the lane and in one corner there was a small tree, fruit of some kind, I thought. At the back, the garden was divided from the field behind by a fence consisting of nothing more than three strands of wire stretching between drunkenly angled posts. This same flimsy fence ran down the left-hand side of the garden until it met a grey wooden lean-to shed. On the right-hand side Tyrrell or some earlier incumbent had put up a more substantial barrier of beaver-boarding down as far as the side of the garage. There was a crazy-paving path leading from the back door up by the side of this fence to the back gate. This area was again mostly grass with one long border close to the house, at present empty of flowers but neatly weeded and raked. This morning the ground was sodden, the clumps of red earth shiny with moisture. There was a smell of wet leaves, and the pebbledash of the cottage was blotched like a map with darker areas of damp. I noticed that the surrounding country was pretty, confirming the impression I'd had looking from my window in the semi-darkness last night. The fields, and the wood on the hill behind the house, looked less menacing, the trees even inviting, surrounded by a tangle of blackberry bushes. Below, sweeping down to the valley the heath land was spattered with buttery-yellow gorse and hazy with mauve heather. Some people were riding across it, at the canter, and I could hear their laughter, faint and brittle like the cry of birds, floating up the hill, and the soft vibration of the horses' hooves was carried to me on the wind. This, I thought, was more like it. This was the country – fresh air, and newly turned earth, and woods, and people riding on the hillside. I felt comforted. I would read for a bit, and then walk, explore, breathe some of that clean air.

The truth was, left to my own devices for those first few days, I did precious little and didn't stray far from the cottage. Apart from the fact that I was exhausted, physically and emotionally, I felt as shy and vulnerable as a wild animal, as though any social interaction, however trivial, was a threat and potentially dangerous. I also had the typical townie's sensation of being watched. Here, where there were far fewer people, those few constituted a potential audience in a way that the anonymous crowds of town never did.

I slept long and often, falling into sleep at odd times and remaining there, dreamless and insensible for hours on end – in bed, on the chair, slumped forward on the table – in a kind of hibernation, or mini-death. One way of looking at it was that I was husbanding my resources for the process of recovery. That may indeed have been part of it, but I now believe that I was in flight, too – fleeing from whatever might be waiting for me out there. I literally didn't trust myself, my senses or perceptions. The problem with madness, I'd often thought, and sometimes discussed with contemporaries in relation to elderly parents and dementia, was that the mad did not recognise it. And I think that's what terrified me most. Was the reality I saw and recognised bending in some way, like a fairground mirror, showing me something that was there, in me, but grotesquely and horribly altered? Sleep, which was always undisturbed, rescued me from all that. Asleep, I was no danger to myself or anybody else.

A couple of times the phone rang, but I didn't answer it. I had told Elise not to call for a few days and there was no one else except Bob (and, I suppose, half the village) who knew I was here. I realised how easy it was, when in a self-imposed exile, to become a recluse. With no routine and no one to answer to I went to bed ludicrously early and was often up at four. Sudden sounds made me jump – the scream of a vixen, the clatter of a pheasant getting up, the sharp rising drone of a car on the road; especially that, I dreaded visitors, but it never happened. I half expected to find the Reverend Thorne beating a path to my door, heaven-bent on swelling his flock, but whether from discretion or idleness he didn't appear.

I walked in the garden, and in the immediately surrounding area. If I so much as saw a figure in the distance I darted back inside and stood in the hall – where I could not be seen through any window – with my heart beating, like a fugitive from justice. My own behaviour humiliated and shamed me. On day three I needed some supplies, but I drove six miles to the supermarket in the neighbouring town rather than brave the village shop with what I perceived as its prying eyes. What a monster of egocentricity I had become.

I needed something to breach this wall of paranoia, and when it came it was in the bracing and garrulous form of Mrs Payne, whose return I had all but forgotten about over these peculiarly timeless few days.

I'd not been up for long, and had been standing in the back garden, safe in the early morning tranquillity. The click of the back gate brought me out in a sweat, but when I saw who it was bustling down the path I got a grip on myself and waited for her by the kitchen door.

'Oh Mr Bowater, I didn't expect you to be up so early – thought I'd cook you some breakfast.'

'That's a very kind thought but I've had some, thank you – I don't have much breakfast anyway.'

She gave me a quick warning look which seemed to say that if I customarily ate a good breakfast I wouldn't be in the mess I was in now, but she refrained from saying anything, and went on ahead of me into the kitchen, removing her headscarf and putting her shopping basket and bag on the table. She looked round as if to see whether I'd made any mark on the place, but all must have looked as it usually did for she made no comment and began to remove the large galoshes she wore over her house shoes.

I said: 'Will I be in your way if I do a little reading for an hour or so? I thought I'd go out for a walk later.'

'You do what you like,' she said, going to one of the cupboards and heaving out a vacuum cleaner and a box of cleaning stuff. 'Just you let me know where you want to sit and I'll do round you.'

'Perhaps for this morning you could just leave the sitting room altogether and I'll go in there.'

'Certainly – you're here for a rest and a rest you shall have.'

I couldn't let that pass. 'A break from routine perhaps, Mrs Payne, and a change, but not a rest. I've got work to do, you know.'

'Of course.' Her tone was indulgent – this was clearly a battle I was doomed to lose. I hovered for a moment, watching her thin, hard red hands dart among the kitchen things, moving, arranging, putting away. She looked over her shoulder at me, with that quick, bird-like movement. 'Shall I make you some coffee around half past ten?'

Time to be diplomatic. 'That would be nice, thank you.'

'You get along and do your reading then,' she said like one addressing a good, if simple, child. And like a child, I obeyed her.

I didn't actually read much. Once installed in one of the armchairs in the empty little sitting room with a pile of books and a notepad, I at once fell into a reverie, watching the clouds drag drifting shadows over the back garden, lulled by the drone of the vacuum cleaner in the upstairs rooms. I pictured Elise, probably sitting over her black coffee reading the morning paper, her silvery hair caught back in a ribbon, not yet out of her night clothes but already discreetly made up, soignée and scented, good enough to eat. I didn't miss her.

College would be empty: just a few members of staff

drifting round like lost souls, studying in the library, talking about their coming holidays, moving studies. The students, by now, would be scattered all over the world – hitching lifts across Europe, bussing across the States, slinging the hash in cafés and hotels, looking after other people's children, arguing with their parents. James had been going to go to Greece.

Although I tried not to I found myself continually imagining his face – as I remembered it and as it must have looked in that lift. How could anyone, *anyone*, cut themselves to death? Hack their arteries with a blade until the life literally seeped out of them, a dark, lake on the glossy parquet? The thought brought the taste of sick into my mouth. And why James? So clever, so poised, so *nice*. Just because he was eighteen and wanted to make love to his tutor's wife? Not possible. I was like Judge Brack with his 'People don't do such things.' When they did, and James had. And I had seen his life pouring out of him long before he had taken it.

God knows I had spent hours, days, trying to explain it away. We all occasionally experience *déjà vu* – we've been here before, seen such and such a face, done such and such a thing in just such a way – but that is after the event. I was conscious of having seen what I saw long before I had any intimation of what it meant. And if I had seen someone else's death, what else might I see . . . ?

I felt the dank crawl of returning depression and stood up sharply to shake it off. I went to the front window and looked over the hedgerows to the common, which was shiny and fresh with rain and distance. I told myself I must look forward, push away the shadows that clung to me like the dusty attic cobwebs that had panicked me as a child. Everything rational, everything academic in me told me it was not possible – I had been depressed, tired, run-down to the point of illness. Who knows what I had seen? A shadow? An imagining? Some morbid intimation of my own mortality? Quite possibly all those things, but why so shockingly real and concrete, the absolute reflection of what was to be?

The awareness that there might be some other mind's eye not guided by the passage of time and the information of memory, was disturbing to say the least. The possibilities that opened were horrific: possibilities of anarchy and lunacy and terror. Where were we, I asked myself, when our notion of order was destroyed?

I felt a light tap on my shoulder and turned to see Mrs Payne, carrying a tray with a mug of coffee, sugar and milk. She must have knocked and entered without my hearing.

'Here's your coffee,' she said.

'Thank you.'

'Do much reading?' She glanced at the blank notepad and the pile of closed books.

'A little.'

'Well, that's the main thing.' She put the tray down and stood watching me with her arms folded, like a guard, as I took the first sip, black and unsweetened.

'Where were you thinking of walking?' she enquired.

'I don't know really – the common over the hill looks nice.'

'Yes, very nice. You can go in a big circle over that way.'

'Perhaps you could give me some directions.' She was obviously keen to do so.

'If you come over here I'll show you.' I took my coffee over to the window and followed her gesturing hand. 'Go down into the lane and turn right – keep going till you come to a gate on your left. There's a footpath round the side of a field, and at the bottom you can get over the bank to the common. Then there's a big cart track right across the middle, Church Path, and it takes you to the village. You can either walk back up, or catch a bus.'

'Oh, I expect I'll walk, it'll do me good – I might have a drink in the pub on my way back.'

'It's not a bad pub,' said Mrs Payne, condemning it utterly with the pursing of her thin mouth. She watched me intently with those dark bird eyes. 'Know many people round here, do you?' I wondered if Tyrrell had made introducing me to the locals part of her brief.

'No, but it doesn't bother me.'

'They're alright on the whole,' she said, as though I had asked. 'We get them all in the shop at one time or another. I reckon I know just about everyone in Ballacombe, it's not a big place. Though to be honest, I'm not a local woman myself, I'm a Londoner, but my Len's a West Countryman and when we got married we decided to get ourselves a little business round here. We do very well – there's no competition you see.'

'Quite. Of course.' There was a brief pause. I drained my coffee and put the mug on the tray. 'Well, I think I'll be off. I expect you'll be gone when I get back.'

'I expect so. I don't come tomorrow, Thursday's my next day, but that'll be the afternoon when the shop closes.'

'Alright, I'll see you then.'

I escaped from Mrs Payne and left the cottage by the front door, turning right at the bottom of the track as she had directed.

It was good to be out. The realities of mud at the side of the road, of puddles and of the sun striking pleasantly on my skin helped to dispel the horrors. A lark twittered, spiralling invisibly into the stratosphere. I walked briskly, making my steps thud on the road, taking deep breaths, swinging my arms unselfconsciously, aware of how foolish I would look if anyone saw me, but confident that they wouldn't.

I had nearly reached the gateway Mrs Payne had mentioned, when I began to get short of breath. I suppose I'd been living a fairly sedentary life, with a certain amount of over-indulgence, and the sudden burst of exercise was a shock to my system. I remembered all the newspaper articles I'd read about businessmen who had coronaries after playing squash and slowed down. But the breathlessness continued, worse if anything. I had to concentrate on each breath, and the air rasped in and out of my lungs painfully. In addition I was feeling faint, the blood going to my stomach. Blurring. By the time I reached the gateway I felt very bad. I literally staggered to the gate and hung there, my legs sagging. My ears were ringing, I was certain I was going to black out, something I'd never done, but somehow I stayed conscious, like a drowning man bobbing near the surface.

Despite the sunshine, the field – lying fallow – looked dark to me. In addition I could see quite clearly what was directly in front of me, though the sides of the picture were indistinct. Into this chiaroscuro came two figures – one quite tall, the other slim and slighter, though both appeared to be men. I tried to call for help, but my throat seemed paralysed and I could manage nothing more than a croak. And now I saw that there was another reason why they didn't hear me – they were fighting. Or at least the larger figure was trying to clutch at the smaller. He succeeded, and for a moment the two of them were locked together. When they burst apart the smaller figure was staggering, falling to its knees. And trancelike, unmoved, as though in a dream, conscious only of my own nausea, I saw the larger man stab the smaller one. Once, twice, repeatedly. It seemed to happen very slowly, as though, had I been well, I could have run from the gate to the centre of the field and stopped the uplifted arm of the killer. As it was, I watched, petrified, by the gate while this extraordinary scene was enacted before me.

Almost as soon as the stabbed man fell to the plough I began to regain strength. My breath came freely, the lightheadedness left me, I could see clearly and brightly. And the field was empty.

The full impact of what I had just witnessed hit me. I looked around wildly for someone to tell – another passer-by, perhaps the killer himself. But the countryside was as bland, and sunny – and empty – as the field in front of me.

Sobbing with fright and shock, I began to climb the gate, awkwardly like a small child. I practically fell over the other side on to the uneven brick-red clods of plough and began to stagger across it, tripping and stumbling as I went, my eyes fixed on the spot – just where the field began to slope away – where I should find the body. I *hoped* I should find that body. I knew what I would do, I would behave sensibly and promptly: cover it with my jacket, go back to the cottage, call police and ambulance, explain that I was a newcomer in the area, perhaps even provide a vital description, though God knows I had seen little enough.

God, oh please, God, let there be something there, let someone have died so I can hang on to my reason.

I reached the place. There was nothing there. There had been nothing there. The rigid ramparts of the furrows were untrodden, though they were so damp that my progress across them had left great potholes in my wake. A blackbird tugging at a worm darted away at my approach, and the lark sang deliriously in heaven. Nothing there. I fell to my knees and ran my hands over the sodden earth as if I should be able to *feel* where that person had fallen. But the ground was cold, clammy, unresponsive. All I could see, in my mind's eye, was my own pathetic figure

– everyman, kneeling in a field, clawing at the ground with his fingers, searching like an animal for his proud intellectual supremacy. Pathetic; and worse, defeated.

I got up, shaking and weak, and began to trail back over the mud to the gate. I was filthy – I must have looked like a tramp. Out of nowhere I thought of Elise and her immaculate beauty. How in God's name was I connected to that woman? Urgently I wiped as much clay as I could from my hands on to my trousers. Then I scrambled over the gate into the lane and stood leaning back, my head sagging, only barely aware of the hum of an approaching car.

Five

'Anything the matter? I say anything the matter?'
I looked up and saw a broad, red face peering solicitously from the rolled down window of a Jag. I must have stared like a zombie – I certainly wasn't capable of any response; my head spun and I was shaking. As it was the man opened the door of the car and stepped out. He probably thought I was a vagrant of some kind – I presumably looked it – for he came a step or two closer and addressed me in the sort of loud, over-deliberate way we use to the simple-minded.

'Something the matter, is there? You don't look well. Can I do anything?' His accent was North Country, an incongruous note which jarred my sense of reality still more. I managed to push myself from the gate and meet his enquiring gaze. I felt I should reply but for some reason I'd completely forgotten what he had asked, so I stood there mouthing like a fish. He peered closely at me.

'You look fit to die, man.' His proximity brought with it a tang of cigar smoke and whisky. His hair was that yellowish white which looks as though it's been stained by nicotine, and his face highly coloured. But his eyes were narrow and blue like a sailor's – vital, piercing eyes. There was something invigorating in his presence that helped to bring me round, like a whiff of salts.

'I'm so sorry, I suddenly felt ill . . .' My voice must

have been a surprise to him for he stepped back almost apologetically, abandoning his masterful air.

'You poor chap.' I saw him glance confusedly at the mud on my clothes.

'I fell over, I must look terrible.'

'Not at all, not at all!' He was all bluff geniality. 'Where are you from? Let me give you a lift.'

'Oh . . .' I didn't think I could face it. 'I shall be alright, I only live up the lane here.'

'Never mind that, you're not fit to walk. Get in the motor and I'll drop you off.'

He was altogether too much for me. I followed docilely and allowed myself to be settled in the comfortable front seat of the Jag. The upholstery was toffee-coloured leather; the car radio was playing easy-listening classics; a fat cigar stub rested in the ashtray. Realities. Trivialities. They were a comfort. I even managed to glance through the window at the field – it was still empty. And it always had been, I told myself firmly, though I didn't believe it.

The big man crashed into the driver's seat, put the cigar butt between large discoloured teeth like a horse's and turned to me.

'Where to?'

'It's called Rook's Cottage – up the lane before the pub on the corner.'

'I know it, I know it.' He started the engine and we glided forward. The car was warm and moved as smoothly as a bird. It reminded me of the Merc, of trips with Elise.

'You're not one of the natives, are you?' enquired the driver.

'No, I'm not. I've borrowed the cottage from a friend for a few months to get some peace and quiet. The name's Michael Bowater.'

'Arnold Deller.' He put his right hand across and shook

mine firmly without taking his eyes from the road. 'Looks as though the peace and quiet doesn't suit you!'

I managed a faint laugh. 'I haven't been here long. It's fine, but I have been overdoing it a bit, you know . . .'

'Yes, yes.' He nodded sagely. 'What's your line when you're at home?'

'I'm a university lecturer in London.'

'Are you, by gum? This it?'

We had drawn level with Rook's Cottage, and the Jag glided to a halt. I began to make my apologies and had my hand on the door handle when he said abruptly, 'Like to come back to my place for a drink, to set you up?' I had begun to refuse politely when I glanced at the cottage. It looked damp and bleak. And empty. What in those square, functional, sparsely furnished little rooms was to keep me from thinking of what I had just seen? Even Mrs Payne had left by now. Just the buzz of the fridge and the cawing of the rooks in the wood at the top of the hill.

'Thank you,' I said. 'I'd like that.'

We drove a little way in silence, turning left at the Lamb and Flag, heading away from the village and climbing slightly, so that we could see the thread of buildings along the main street of Ballacombe in the dip below us to the right. Suddenly my Samaritan remarked, 'I'm retired myself, from up north – Leeds.'

'I thought you didn't sound like a local.'

'Sticks out like a spare prick, doesn't it?' He laughed a great braying noisy laugh, rolling the cigar to the side of his mouth. I liked him.

'Yes,' he went on, 'I'd have stayed where I belong but the wife always fancied the West Country. And there were other things. Family problems you know . . .' He gave me a man-to-man look and I nodded understandingly. 'Our girl, Susan, wasn't happy,' he added and then, as if changing the subject: 'How are you feeling now, you don't look quite so pasty.'

'I'm better, thank you. I just felt faint and fell – it gave me a shock, that was all. I suppose I'd been overdoing it more than I'd realised.'

'It keeps you busy does it, lecturing?' I sensed an almost involuntary disparagement – the tough self-made businessman looking at the effete academic.

'There's quite a bit of strain attached to it,' I said, and then, making myself say it: 'A student I particularly admired committed suicide.'

'Jesus H. Christ!' He sounded genuinely shocked. 'What a tragedy.'

'It was. And he chose a particularly unpleasant method – slashed his wrists . . .'

'That's terrible. Terrible.' He seemed so sincerely moved, even chastened, that I warmed to him still more. We relapsed into silence, both of us with our own view of old, unhappy far-off things, until the Jag swung into a well-kept white gravel drive flanked by red-brick gate posts.

'Here we are,' said Deller, and there was a note of pride in his voice. I could see why. The Deller residence was large, new, opulent and, if not beautiful, at least so obviously the fruits of prosperity that one could only stand back and admire.

'We built it ourselves,' he told me. 'I said, when we retire, we're going to be bloody comfortable and no messing. And I saw to it.'

'It's a fine house.'

'It is, and it's not just a pretty face either – it's got every mod con and then some. When I had the business I was always too busy to enjoy my money. I thought, when I retire I'm buggered if I'll stint myself.'

'Quite right.'

We got out of the car and scrunched across the gravel

to the doorway, which was flanked by whitewashed pillars inscribed with the words 'Deller House', one on either side. The rest of the house was red brick, picked out in white, in a neo-Georgian style. Probably in time it would be a truly fine house, acquire dignity and character. Now it was a little too new and stark, sitting up here on the hillside with its bright new face shining brashly in the sun.

The door was ajar and we went in. He was right, the house was comfortable. The temperature was tropical, even on the late August morning, and everything spoke of newness – the carpet was thick and pale, and the wallpaper, in a similar colour, was flocked in a way that reminded me of Chinese restaurants but which was nonetheless sumptuous. The walls were partly panelled in a light wood which had been highly polished. On them, and on the two exquisite antique tables which stood on either side of the hall, were hung or placed numerous carefully chosen *objets* – Chinese vases, a Victorian barometer, a huge burnished copper urn, one or two good Picasso prints, over-elaborately framed. Everything had been carefully selected, and was good of its kind – but there was rather too much of it. I chastised myself for being so snobbishly critical and wished I had the money to make such mistakes.

Deller called, 'Marjorie! Come and meet someone.'

'Coming.' The voice was from upstairs. I suddenly caught sight of my reflection in a mirror.

'Good God, look at me,' I said. 'I can't let your wife see me like this, and heaven knows what I'm doing to your carpet.'

'Get away with you. Marge'll give you a brush for your trousers, and you can have a wash if you want. Take your shoes off if you like, they look wet any road.'

Deller was so friendly and hospitable that I should dearly have liked to tell him my worries. It would have been a comfort just to hear him sweep them aside. But now was not the time. Marjorie Deller came running down the stairs.

She was a small, vivacious woman in her forties, and I could see what must have attracted Deller – she had a sassy, smart glamour – not Elise's cool chic, but something more robust, and perhaps more attractive to most men. A well-set-up, well-turned-out woman, now slightly plump where once she'd been buxom, and slightly brassy where once she'd been blonde, but her eyes were warm, and her handshake firm. I liked her instantly.

'How do you do, Mr Bowater,' she said, on being introduced to me. 'You poor thing, you must be soaked. Come and I'll show you where you can wash and brush up – would you like a pair of Arnold's slippers?'

'That's very kind – but I mustn't stay long.'

'You're staying long enough to get dry and have a drink, so there. Come on upstairs and I'll show you where.' She flashed me a slightly flirtatious smile. Deller took his cue.

'And if you're not down in five minutes, woman, I'll come looking for you.' Both of them laughed loudly and I followed Marjorie upstairs. On the first floor the same opulence prevailed, but the colour scheme had changed from cream and gold to deep blue. The bathroom I was ushered into – 'the guest bathroom' – was turquoise and fitted out in the full film star monty with shell-shaped bath and jacuzzi, a telephone stuck to the wall, acres of poodle-wool carpeting and a phalanx of blue glass bottles filled with powder, lotion, bath salts and the like – Penhaligon's Bluebell, like as not.

'Give me those shoes and I'll get our man to scrape them and put them on the boiler. You get clean and come down when you're ready, I'll have some slippers for you downstairs, and –' she winked like a cheery barmaid – 'a stiff drink. Whisky?'

'That would be marvellous. You're very kind.'

'Away with you.' Still smiling to herself, she pulled the door to and left me to it. As I scrubbed the clay from under my nails and combed my hair I thought of how Elise would criticise these people's taste. Not to their faces, of course, she was always polite, but how she would laugh at their cockle-shell pretensions and Chinese-restaurant walls after we'd gone. All that money! she would say, and no idea how to spend it. The more I was away from her, the less I liked her.

As I went down the stairs, quiet in my stockinged feet, I stopped on the half landing to look out of the vast floor-to-ceiling window. The view was superb, right out over the drive and front garden, over Ballacombe down in the dip, to the rolling hills and fields beyond. I went on down, saw my hosts through an open door and joined them in a huge drawing room that extended across the full width of the house.

'What a great view you have,' I said, as Marjorie bustled over with slippers and Scotch.

'Oh yes,' she said, 'this house was built for that view. It's so lovely, it quite takes my breath away every time I look at it – but it's best from the upstairs windows, the hedge gets in the way down here.'

'Look at my garden,' said Deller, taking my elbow and leading me to the French window. 'Not bad, eh?'

It was indeed not bad, although like the house its brand spanking newness was almost too harsh. Blocks of flowers lay like mosaic patterns in the borders, the grass was as smooth as a putting green, and beyond a rose trellis about a hundred yards from the house I could just make out the burgeoning greenness of the vegetable garden. Two figures stood in the archway that led from lawn to vegetable garden framed by the trellis work – they looked like dolls on a wedding cake in that setting. Deller must have seen where my gaze rested, for he said: 'That's my gardener and our girl, Susan – she loves to grow things, they're always chatting about plants and seeds and so on, you'd never know she was a city girl.' He looked over his shoulder to his wife: 'Give Susan a call, love, she'd want to meet Mr Bowater.'

'If you like. She's a bit shy,' said Marjorie to me confidentially, 'a bit backward in coming forward if you know what I mean – you mustn't mind.'

'Of course he won't.' Deller sounded quite sharp, but his wife seemed to take it in good part. When I glanced back at him he seemed a little embarrassed.

'Marge is right, she is a shy girl, but I see no cause to apologise.'

'Of course not. It makes a pleasant change nowadays.'

'She's going on twenty-five,' he said, as though I had asked. 'It's hard to bring up a girl right without protecting them too much.'

'Of course.' I sensed something unsaid in the air, something that my host might have added, in different circumstances. I thought: Perhaps when we know each other better I may tell him, he may tell me . . .

We heard Marjorie's voice calling, and one of the figures in the garden lifted a hand in a small wave and began to walk back across the lawn to the house. Deller went to refill our glasses and I watched as Susan approached. She didn't look nearly twenty-five, she wore an old green gabardine mac with no belt, and Wellingtons, for the ground was still sodden after last night's downpour. Her hair, straight and dark, was bobbed, but not very well – a straggly version of what Elise would have called a pudding-basin. Between the low hem of the mac and the top of the boots I saw that she wore corduroy trousers. When she had almost reached the house, she looked up at the window but, meeting my stare, looked away again quickly and bounded up the steps.

In a couple of minutes she entered, accompanied by Marjorie. Seeing her closer, I was immediately struck by her beauty. It shone through her dowdy clothes and poor haircut – and was only enhanced by the fact that she wore no make-up. She had a strong, rather boyish face, and I could see a lot of her father in the set of her chin and fine shape of her head. Her eyes were brown, with strongly marked black brows that stood out against the pallor of her skin. Only her mouth was soft – large, curved and sensual, a provocative mouth. All this combined with her tallness – she was about my height – and her complete lack of sophistication made her appearance disturbing, and fascinating. Marjorie introduced her to me and she gave my hand a firm shake.

'How do you do.' Her voice was soft and light and her movements gauche, but she looked me straight in the eye. I could see what her outgoing sociable mother meant by her 'shyness' and yet to me it seemed more like a kind of quiet defiance. She warned you with those eyes: 'Keep off. Don't pry.' She had a peculiar composure all her own. While Deller, affectionately circling her shoulders with his arm, told her about me I had a chance to observe the family as a group. It seemed to me, as an outsider, that the parents, for all their extrovert sociability, were the nervous ones. But nervous about what? I thought: Everyone has a secret which would vanish if they could tell it, but they're afraid to tell.

Susan turned to me: 'Are you better now?'

'Yes, thank you, it was just a funny turn.'

'Good.' She sat down as if that ended the matter. Man on his own, not eating properly, she must have thought.

'A drink, love?' Deller hovered over her.

'No, thanks, Dad.' She sat composedly, her fingers linked, hanging between her knees. I thought if this girl knew how to dress, how to present herself, the world would be at her feet. And yet part of her charm, her mystery, lay in her oddness. I asked: 'What do you do – I mean do you work down here?'

'No.' She shook her head, glanced down at her hands, seemed about to add something but thought better of it. Marjorie said: 'She was at college doing a BTEC till last year. She's trying to decide, aren't you, love?'

'That's right.'

'I hear you like gardening,' I pressed on. 'I must say your garden here is superb. I'm a Londoner and no expert, but I should think this is a showpiece by any standards.'

'It is beautiful, isn't it?' She smiled for the first time. 'And we made it all from scratch.'

'Don't get the idea I had much to do with it,' said Deller. 'Holz and Susan worked like a couple of slaves. I wrote the cheques, but they did it.'

'Holz?'

'My gardener.'

'That's never an old Devonshire name.'

'No, he was a German POW. Stayed on, but never married. You must come out when you've another drink, meet him and take a closer look at his handiwork.'

'I'd like to.'

'You and Holz get on like a house on fire, don't you?' said Deller to his daughter jovially, but I sensed another dimension to the question. She only nodded and he turned to me, as though answering for her: 'They've got such a set of green fingers between them I reckon they could grow daffs in the Sahara – it's a real shared passion.'

'Yes, but Dad,' said Susan with an air of honourable embarrassment, 'he's a genius, I'm just keen.'

'He works, I'll say that for him.'

'He's a funny man though,' said Marjorie, addressing herself to me. 'He's been in this country nearly thirty years, but do you know he's still like a stranger. Doesn't talk to anyone much, and he's still got a strong accent after all this time. I don't think English folk are stuffy – think of all the Germans who stayed here after the war, and they've been accepted. But I must be honest, that man's not liked round here.'

'People always mistrust a loner,' I ventured.

'That's true but it's as though he doesn't want to get to know the locals – holds himself aloof, almost scornful.'

'I like him,' said Susan, in her quiet voice, as though talking to herself. But she had an alert, almost jumpy audience in her father.

'I know you do, girl. And I've got nothing against the man. It's just that if he's got nothing to hide—'

'Of course he doesn't!'

'I say, if he has nothing to hide there's more he could do to help himself.'

'If he has nothing to hide he shouldn't have to.'

Deller shook his head at her naivety. 'Human nature doesn't change. People think, no smoke without a fire. They need stopping. It may not be fair, but that's folks.'

'It's horrible.'

I felt that an exchange familiar to the participants, though not to me, was being played out for the umpteenth time. The air buzzed. Susan's face was flushed, her expression highly charged – I was reminded, with brutal clarity and suddenness, of James. To cover my own emotion, I asked: 'What do people say about Holz?'

Susan dropped her head, picking at her trousers in that childlike way, avoiding everyone's eye, opting out of the conversation as abruptly as she'd charged in. Deller slapped me on the shoulder, but his manner was no less awkward.

'Oh, you know villages . . . good rumour's meat and drink to them.'

My heart sank. 'I've heard that.'

He laughed, too heartily. 'Better watch yourself, man of mystery, stranger in town. You could take the heat off Holz in no time. Probably already have.'

'Excuse me.' Susan rose and left the room, closing the door softly behind her.

'Anyway,' said Deller. 'Tell me, d'you like golf?'

'I'm afraid not.' I thought of Bob Tyrell, whose passion golf was.

'No matter, you'll like the club. Why don't you join us for lunch there after my round on Saturday? Marge generally comes over, don't you, sweet?'

'Thank you.' I couldn't think of an excuse, and they were obviously the sort of people who railroaded others with hospitality. Goodhearted but overbearing, they simply assumed compliance: I was in what's known as an opt-out situation, and opting out would involve more energy and quicker thinking than I was capable of.

'One o'clock, at the club then, it's a date.'

'Where is the club?'

'Don't worry, I'll pick you up at quarter to,' said Marjorie. They were unstoppable. 'Arnold'll tell me where.'

'Right then—!' He slapped his big hands together. 'Come on, down that drink and I'll show you round the estate. Don't mind about the slippers.'

'Oh. Thank you.' I gulped the last of my Scotch and followed him out of the French window. We went down some steps, across a patio, more steps, and we were on the lawn, the marks of the mower stretching straight and immaculate as tramlines down to the trellis.

As we walked round the well-kept borders Deller kept up a running commentary, most of which, not being much of a horticulturalist, I didn't understand, but attempted to make the right noises. At one point he took me to the side of the garden where a low wall fell away on the other side, revealing a view of the common, and even the neat grey roof of Rook's Cottage just visible over the swell of the hillside. I could also see the ploughed field, like a square red hankie against the green, brown and gold of the land. A little breeze got up and chased up the hill towards us, rippling the yellowish grass, making me shiver although it was past midday and the sun was high. Deller pointed out landmarks. 'Church Path, across the common there, do you know it?'

'My daily woman told me about it. I was going to walk there when I had my funny turn.'

'You must, it's quite historic I believe. The church at Ballacombe used to be the parish church for a huge area round here – it's the oldest one in these parts as you'll notice if you're here for long. That path used to be the cross-country route to the church, everyone went that way – weddings, processions, funerals – it dates back centuries, though most of it's been blotted out now except for that stretch. Some old maps show its original route: it used to cut through that little wood above your place and come down where that cart track is now, just by your gate. Then along the line of the lane, across the fields—'

'Where the plough is?'

'About there, yes. Across the fields and over the common land to the village. Miles it must have gone back beyond the wood, and there were other ways too from the other villages, but I only know of that one – it's the only church path you can still see.'

'That's interesting.' The little breeze whispered around us; the country lay tranquil as a sleeping child. I asked quickly: 'Can we look at the rest of the garden? I mustn't impose on you much longer.'

'It's no imposition!' Deller put a hand on my shoulder and we walked across the grass, through the arch in the trellis work into the vegetable garden. The gardener was digging in one of the beds, but he looked up and raised a hand as we approached. Deller called: 'Holz! Come and meet a visitor from London, he's been admiring your handiwork.'

His robust use of the man's surname made me uncomfortable, but the gardener thrust his fork into the soil, wiped his hands on his dungarees and came over. He was tall and straight, with a deliberate, dignified air.

'Here he is,' said Deller jovially, 'the man who makes the garden grow – Holz, this is Michael Bowater, staying at Rook's Cottage.' The German's face was long and aquiline, an intelligent but rather humourless face. The dark hair was brushed straight back, the eyes were deep set and intense. He had the sallow, blue-chinned complexion of an actor or writer, someone whose life was indoors rather than out in all weathers. His hand when I shook it was cold, hard and callused, but the fingers were long and delicate as a musician's.

'How do you do.' He was soft-spoken with a marked accent. He stood looking at us politely as if waiting for one of us to dismiss him.

I found his presence slightly embarrassing and wondered what his position had been before the war – not a gardener surely. I could readily understand something of what the villagers thought, but I was ashamed of it. To cover what I was sure was an obvious awkwardness I said: 'It's amazing what you've done here – and all from scratch.'

'Thank you.'

'I'm no gardener, so I can't give an informed opinion, but I think Mr Deller has just cause for pride.'

'I think so.' His lack of fake modesty, or deference, discomforted me. There was a kind of quiet defiance or perhaps self-reliance about him which reminded me of Susan Deller. No wonder, I thought, they get on – they're two of a kind. Deller asked, employer to employee: 'You were here early this morning.'

'Well, I couldn't do much yesterday. The rain . . . so I decided to catch up today.'

'Good man. But don't hang about late this afternoon.'

'I'll finish the jobs.'

'Of course, of course. Thanks.' We parted, Deller whispering earnestly to me that the fellow was a worker in a million, a real enthusiast, a dedicated man.

I cast a glance over my shoulder at Holz as we walked back. He had heaved the big gardening fork from the earth and was plunging it into a new area. Something about the action, the tall thin figure, the shape of the long head, struck a chord. I had seen it before. And as we reached the house I believed I remembered where.

I had just seen my murderer again. And he had been digging a potato patch all morning.

Six

The meeting with the Dellers must have done me good, because the shock didn't quite take hold as it had done before, with James's death or the incident of the bookshop, let alone the horror of this morning. It might have been the drink, or the ordinary social intercourse, the knowledge that I could converse and behave properly, that I was not in their eyes a lunatic – but I managed, I don't quite know how, to remain calm. After Deller had run me back to Rook's Cottage and I was sitting with a glass of claret and a background of Sibelius on the radio I realised (and this was quite shocking in itself) that I was getting used to it. Becoming accustomed to the idea that I had some strange gift or propensity. That I saw things: that I was vouchsafed information not available to others. It was neither pleasant nor comfortable, but I was beginning to accept it.

And with acceptance dawned a second realisation – that if I, for some strange and mysterious reason, was the repository of privileged information, I had also had bestowed on me the responsibility for acting upon it.

Two evenings later, Elise phoned.

'Hallo, Michael.'

'Elise.'

'I phoned to find out how you were. I didn't like to before – I thought you might be tired.'

'Tyrrell had no such considerations.'

'Oh! I told him not to.'

'It was kindly meant. He's set everything up very nicely for me down here.'

'And how are you – how are you really?'

'Well, it hasn't been long. Still I think it'll suit – I've had my bleak moments, but I expect that was all the driving yesterday. I'm not up to anything at the moment.'

'What do you mean, bleak moments?'

'I felt a bit faint. But I met some extremely kind people as a result.'

'It all seems masochistic to me.'

'Well, perhaps it is a little. But I need a purge, a wrench, something to stop me getting further in—'

'And that's another thing, it's not as if I know what the matter is exactly. I've never felt more superfluous in my life, people keep asking me . . .'

'I'm sorry.'

After a short pause she said, 'Look, why don't you come back to town?'

I was staggered by her arrogance. 'Elise, I've only just got here, I haven't given it a chance.'

'Yes, I know that. I'm asking you to change your mind. Why not let's see if we can't make you better between us.' An olive branch, a hand across the abyss. This was what I had been wanting for years, the chance to break down the barrier, admit our mutual dependence, let the defences down. Why then did I instinctively resist it?

'I don't know . . . I think the reasons I came here still hold good.'

'It's extraordinary. Uncivilised.' She was sharp.

'Not so extraordinary. Everyone has to take stock from time to time.'

'But not away from their wives. A wife is to help, isn't she?'

'You have been a help.' Even to myself I sounded

fatuous, implausible, but I stumbled on. 'Being here on my own has nothing to do with you, personally, my darling. It's not that I need to be away from you – but that I need to be on my own.'

'It's not as if you are any better – you've been feeling ill. What happens if you are ill at night, on your own?'

'I have a telephone.'

'And if you black out?'

'I shan't—' I was about to deny it, but something caught at my sleeve, and I concluded: 'That's unlikely.'

'When will you be coming back?'

'I'd like to give it a month, at least. Besides, I shall be reading. It's a good chance to do some research.'

'A month is a long time. It'll be winter when you come back.' She made it sound like a threat.

'Good heavens, scarcely – what does it matter any-way?'

'Oh, never mind, I just hoped we could – achieve something. For a change.'

'We already have – we're the only happily married couple we know. Everyone envies me.' I only dared the hypocrisy because I knew she would not refute it.

'Don't be so sentimental.'

'Oh, for God's sake, Elise, what do you want?'

'I don't know. I thought – that you might.'

'Now who's being sentimental?'

There was a long silence. There seemed nothing else to say. I hadn't even got the measure of myself. I was confused by my own behaviour as much as by Elise's. When I heard the small, distant click of the phone being put down it seemed unreal. I held the phone for a full minute after Elise had gone, listening to the hum of the line, staring blankly out of the window. I thought: I can't leave here, something's going to happen and only I can stop it. Then I put the receiver down with a crash and cursed myself for my stupidity. I was ill, tired, nervous, I'd had a hallucination. Yet I was stupid enough to reject an offer of help and company – from my wife, who actually owed it to me – preferring to be here alone with my signs, portents, ghosts – whatever they were.

I sank down in a chair. It was eight o'clock and darkening, but I didn't turn the light on. I thought: If this was a hallucination, what about James? That, too? I had not been ill then, yet what I saw happened exactly as I'd seen it – almost as though I'd willed it. And this, today, had been clearer, in broad daylight, in a place I hardly knew, away from all associations and memories. And then Holz . . . I had not been aware of seeing the 'killer' clearly and yet when I had turned in the Dellers' garden and seen that tall figure plunging, stabbing, with the fork, his sharp profile pointing to the ground, I had known that this was him. Was it perhaps after all a case of *déjà vu* – that feeling of 'I've been here before, seen these things in this way' when in fact it was merely a double take, that one had seen them not weeks, but seconds, before. But no, for I had been faint, had run across the field, had fallen to my knees and got my clothes and hands covered in red mud. Deller had picked me up in the very spot. I *had* seen a killing, while the man I watched was digging a garden two miles away. What was happening to me? Despite my depression and confusion I did not feel I was going mad. To go mad was to 'take leave of one's senses' and yet I knew mine had never been sharper. Everything was keenly experienced. I had the sensation of being at the centre of a web, attached to various points by fine, almost invisible threads, sensitive to every movement. I was aware of the Dellers in the big house on the hill, of Elise and Tyrrell in London, of the red-faced vicar at Glebe House, of Mrs Payne at her newsagents . . . all somehow at my fingertips.

I heard a loud rustling in the front garden and went

to the window. Because there were no lights on in the cottage I was accustomed to the twilight and could see pretty well. A quick, low shadow moved across the grass, up towards the cottage. It passed very close to the window and then stopped. It was a fox, his russet fur reduced to grey along with the rest of the evening world. His great sensitive ears pricked like radar scanners, I could almost feel the vibration of his whole body as he sniffed, listened, peered. He knew he was being watched. I experienced an odd sense of power. Here was this wild, nocturnal animal, standing no more than a few feet from me, conscious of something, but unable with all his instinct and cunning to detect what. Probably for the only time in my life I had the edge over a wild animal.

For about a minute he stood poised, and I watched. Then, as abruptly as he had stopped, he trotted off, trailing his heavy brush a few inches above the path, and giving one quick, suspicious little look over his shoulder as though fearing he might be followed.

I turned on the light, and blotted out the garden with blackness.

On Saturday, Marjorie zoomed up in a small purple car of the kind expressly designed with the woman driver in mind – a cute car, one might almost have said cuddly. I predicted a state-of-the-art stereo and a sun roof but no leg room.

I was watching for her and went out at once. She leaned across and pushed open the passenger door, beaming.

'Hop in.'

'Good morning. This is very good of you.'

'Nonsense. Excuse the runaround, I know it's not what you're used to.'

'Actually,' I said, 'this is a very nice car.'

It was, surprisingly spacious inside, with comfortable seats and a sensible, user-friendly dashboard.

'Glad you approve!' She was teasing me, a touch flirtatiously, for patronising her. 'It does me a treat.' She turned on to the main road with a flourish. 'Arnold calls it "the hairdrier".'

'So who's he playing golf with?' I asked as we hummed up through the gears to a somewhat injudicious 75 mph.

'Oh, he has a couple of cronies up there,' she chuckled. 'But don't worry, they won't be joining us.'

'It hadn't occurred to me,' I lied, because actually I hadn't relished the thought of being thrown into company with a bunch of golf-fanatics. I was no sportsman, and unclubbable with it. 'Is Arnold a good player?'

She nodded, adding without rancour: 'He should be, he practises enough.'

'Do you play?'

'I know how to, which is *not* the same thing. And I don't want to get into all that lady members nonsense – doing the flowers in the lounge and keeping out of sight six days out of seven.'

I was getting to like Marjorie more with every moment. Arnold Deller was a lucky man.

'So how do you fill your days?' I asked, and was immediately worried in case she thought that once again I was being condescending. But characteristically she took the question in the right spirit.

'Very easily, with that great barn of a place to look after. And there's still a lot left to do in the way of decorating and getting things right. I like home-making.' She flashed me that warm, bright look. 'And I was born with the knack. There aren't that many of my sort left, I should hire out by the hour.'

The golf club was on the edge of the market town where I'd done my first, fugitive, supermarket shop; I remembered driving past it. The surroundings were lovely – no wonder these places were expensive to join – softly rolling countryside, brought lovingly and sensitively under control in the service of the sport. But it was the clubhouse which was the real surprise – not the single-storey pavilion I'd expected, but a perfectly splendid Edwardian house with an imposing entrance and high, grand, well-decorated rooms; fresh flowers (I remembered Marjorie's remark) and a restaurant to do the heart good, with widely spaced tables, crisp white cloths, sparkling glass and a delightful view over the manicured ninth to the rough and woods beyond.

Arnold was waiting for us at a window table, alone, as his wife had predicted. It was at once evident that he was a valued member, because chairs were drawn back, menus and wine list brought, napkins discreetly placed and a waiter hovered, all, it seemed, within seconds.

We ordered from the set menu – whitebait and noisettes of lamb for me, soup ('I like a good soup and they do a good one') and steak and kidney pie for Arnold, and two starters, whitebait and smoked chicken salad, for Marjorie. A bottle of white burgundy arrived and Arnold tasted it and nodded appreciatively. For the first time in longer than I could remember I felt relaxed, hungry – normal.

'Did you win?' I asked.

'I played alright. Not a classic round, but workman-like.'

'Marjorie's been telling me how good you are.'

'She understands a wife's duties,' he said without a smile but drolly. 'That's why I picked her.'

He obviously wasn't about to expand on the morning's golf, so I asked more generally: 'Don't you find it quiet in a place like this after Leeds? I have to say, for me there's something almost as claustrophobic about the peace of the country as there is about the noise of town.'

'You're just not used to it,' said Marjorie, '– is he? We were a bit like that at first.'

Arnold agreed. 'But we've never been busier.'

They didn't quite understand my point. 'I can see you've made a life. But of course I'm not doing that. I came down here to clear my mind, and then perversely found there aren't enough distractions. So far,' I added, in case I seemed unappreciative.

'It'll be doing you good,' he said, 'even if you've got the heebie-jeebies just now. Where we're concerned, a bit of quiet's what we came for, and what we got. And we like to support the goings-on in the village, join in, do our bit. There's plenty to do if you care to.'

The good wine and congenial atmosphere made me bold. 'What about Susan? I wouldn't have thought there was much for an intelligent girl of her age around here.'

The food arrived and Marjorie watched her plate, staying out of it.

'No,' said Arnold, 'but then she is the quiet type. Don't know where she gets it from.'

'As long as she's got the garden,' put in Marjorie, 'she's happy. She's never been one for clothes and shops and whatnot.'

There was the minutest pause, only awkward because these were usually the easiest people in the world.

'Whitebait alright?' asked Arnold.

'Delicious.'

'Too fiddly for me, an excuse for a fish, but each to his own.'

'Do you have a family?' asked Marjorie.

'I'm married,' I told her, thinking how incredibly far away all that seemed, another world, another life, another me . . . 'But we don't have any children.'

'Don't fret about it,' said Arnold bluntly, in case I might

have been. 'They're a blessing and a curse. I never thought I was a worrier, but my Lord—!'

'You're as soft as muck with that girl,' said Marjorie, gently. She gave me a wry glance. 'To look at him you'd think he was tough, but oh, no.'

'I've heard this. About fathers and daughters generally, I mean.'

'He's the worst.' Now she laid her hands in her lap, beaming. 'Tell me about your wife.'

I did. For the next half an hour or so I revived that pleasant sensation of singing Elise's praises, my eulogy borne out by the photograph that I carried in my wallet.

'Oh, but she's a beauty!' cried Marjorie, while Arnold contented himself with a tactful 'very nice' as if she were a car or a house. After that, the amiable interrogation went on to my job and so on and though I was careful for their sake and mine to skirt round the immediate reason for my presence down here, it was somehow comforting to be drawn out, to be wrapped in the warm blanket of their friendly interest.

Lunch was excellent, and after a stroll along the edge of the fairway it was three thirty before we left. Marjorie went off a little ahead of us in the runaround and I travelled back in state with Arnold.

Like many a driver of a performance car he didn't push it but cruised gently, aware that he could overtake and leave for dead any other vehicle on the road if he so chose. The weather turned and became grey and drizzly as it had been on my arrival in Ballacombe. As we drove down the hill towards the village my mood dipped too – back to loneliness and my habitual thoughts and peculiarities. Oddly, Arnold, the least likely candidate imaginable for telepathy, seemed to pick up on this and said apropos of nothing: 'What we were saying about my chap Holz . . . there's more to it than just prejudice.'

'Oh?' I felt an icy trickle of apprehension.

'I'm not saying there's any truth in any of it, either, mind, just that if there's someone who doesn't quite fit in, people will put two and two together and make five.'

I waited. The first austere little houses of Ballacombe slid by; the windscreen was dotted with rain.

'To be honest, Bowater, you might not think it but this place has a past.'

'I'd be disappointed if it didn't,' I said, trying to josh him out of it. 'A suitably gruesome one, I hope, littered with plagues, witch-hunts and incest.'

'All that,' he grunted, turning up the lane towards Rook's Cottage. 'And the rest.'

I waited again. We reached the house and I thought perhaps he'd changed his mind, but when he'd switched the engine off he sat with his hands still on the steering wheel, arms braced, apparently in a world of his own.

'Thank you so much for that excellent lunch,' I said, assuming I was being dismissed. 'You must let me return the compliment some time. For now, would you like to come in and have a coffee? Or something stronger, a chaser perhaps . . . ?'

He shook his head, I suspected as much at his own thoughts as my invitation. I'd actually begun to open the car door when he said abruptly: 'A few years back, just after we got here, a young girl disappeared. Just vanished –' he snapped his fingers – 'without trace.'

I drew the door shut as gently as I could. 'That's terrible. Shocking in such a small place. You read about these things in the papers . . .'

'Yes. The whole village was knocked for six. Waiting for the body to turn up, you know . . .' He shot me a look, checking that he had my attention. He need not have worried about that. The hairs, not just on the back of my neck, but on my forearms, were erect.

'And did it?'

'No. Everyone held their breath, prepared themselves for the worst. We all know the scum that's out there and what they can do . . .' He squeezed the steering wheel as if squeezing a windpipe. 'But nothing. No end to it. They even closed the case for lack of evidence. Family moved away.'

'But, as you say . . . it's not over.'

'Can't be. How could it be?' He jerked his head towards the rain-blurred hill beyond the cottage. 'She could still be out there. Her body, I mean. Anyway,' – his tone became more matter-of-fact – 'people like someone to blame, and if they're not given a culprit they'll go out and find one.'

'Holz,' I said.

'You can understand why – loner, foreigner, bit aloof, bit superior—'

'The old enemy,' I ventured.

'I'm glad you said that.'

'It's bound to be a factor, anywhere. These things die hard.'

'You're right there.'

'And – what do you think?'

'I think they're wrong.' He gave me another hard, emphatic look. 'Very wrong.'

'So you went out on a limb employing Holz.'

'Oh, don't go getting any ideas about charity. I don't do charity. In my opinion he was the best man for the job, and nothing's happened to change my mind. Innocent until proved guilty, all that.'

'The trouble with trial by rumour,' I said, 'is that it never reaches a conclusion.'

He gave a short, angry laugh. 'That's true. So tell me –' he seemed to relax a little – 'what did you think of him?'

'Me? I only met him for a moment or two.'

'Gut reactions are often the best.'

'I thought he was – impressive.'

'Impressive. Good word, yes.'

'And dignified. Perhaps that's what some people mistake for an air of superiority.'

'You're right, dammit.' He seemed disproportionately pleased with this endorsement and vindication of his own feelings. 'You're dead right. Holz is an odd one, but straight as a die, I felt it in my water right away.'

I could tell that the conversation, as far as he was concerned, was at an end, but there was something I felt compelled to add.

'He struck me as unusual in all kinds of ways, actually. Which made it all the odder that I had the strong sense that I'd seen him before.'

'The *déjà vu*, it often happens,' agreed Arnold, quite cheerily now. 'They say it's all a trick of the light, don't they?'

'Yes, but in this instance—' I was about to tell him every-thing, confide in him, describe what I had just experienced when he picked me up, bedraggled and distraught in the road. But nothing kills a confidence quicker than boredom and I could see, suddenly, that if not bored he was at least impatient to be gone. He'd raised a difficult topic and it had been dealt with to his satisfaction.

'Thanks again for your hospitality,' I said, getting out. 'I'll be in touch.'

'Or you'll answer to my wife!'

I watched the big car turn and purr back down the lane. I was glad not to have said more, and scared off my new acquaintances. But the sense of having been handed a gift which, like Deller's depiction of children was also a curse, lay heavy on me as I unlocked the door of my silent, soulless house.

The following day I managed to do some reading, and was undisturbed, for Mrs Payne did not call. I didn't go out except to walk to the pub in the early evening. It was empty, and after one pint I returned to a bowl of soup and the radio till nine thirty when I went to bed. The days slipped by and on Thursday, I awoke feeling for the first time rested, and glad to be in the country. My experience of the first day, while still undeniably real, had lost some of its horror. I was, for the moment, fatalistic. I decided to go down into the village, collect a few items of shopping that I needed, and to locate Mrs Payne's place of work in order to give her a lift up to the cottage. She would be up in the afternoon, as it was early closing, and I knew the bus service still left a lot of walking. Anyway, it did no harm to ingratiate myself.

I parked the Morris in one of the side roads leading off the wide high street and began to walk – uphill, for I began by Glebe House where I had dropped the vicar my first evening in Ballacombe. This time there were more people about – frighteningly young girls with permed hair and laddered stockings, pushing prams; a few elderly people shuffling along, their eyes fixed on something in their imaginations, carrying baskets containing one loaf, one packet of frozen fish; a policeman; some local men, talking on the pavement.

I eventually located L.E. Payne, Newsagent, Confectioner, Tobacconist, at the top of the hill where the high street began to level out. It was a small, dark shop, with the accent quite definitely on the sweets and fags rather than the reading matter. It was empty and I went straight to the counter. It was Mrs Payne herself who emerged from a room at the back and greeted me cheerfully.

'Hallo, Mr Bowater, what can I do for you?'

'I have some things to do in the village – I thought I might have a sandwich in the pub and then give you a lift to Rook's Cottage this afternoon – save you the bus?'

'Well, I must say that's very kind. We close here at one today.'

'I remember you telling me. I'll call round at about half past – will that give you time?'

'I have to give Len his dinner . . .'

'Of course, of course – quarter to two?'

'That'd be fine.'

As I left the shop I heard her say, as she returned to the back room, 'That's him . . .' I wondered what she thought of me. I felt certain that Bob Tyrrell was the apple of her eye – he probably seemed to her to be all that a 'gentleman' should be – amiable, cultured, beneficent, full of 'old chaps' and 'by Gods'. In fact the very things that irritated me in my friend would be virtues in her eyes. I must seem a poor specimen after him.

I went on up the village, enjoying being an observer. I did my bit of shopping, eschewing the dark and dusty village shop in favour of a small supermarket franchise. As I emerged, a voice behind me said: 'Hallo, again!'

It was the garrulous vicar, Cyril Thorne. He did not seem quite so huge divested of his oilskin cape, but his face was as bluff and rosy as ever, and his handshake hearty.

'Where are you heading?' he asked.

'Nowhere in particular, just taking a look at the village, doing some shopping – thought I might have a pint in the Lamb and Flag, will they do a sandwich there?'

'Yes, not too bad – I'm going that way. May I walk with you?'

We fell into step up the high street. Thorne nodded and smiled at various people as we walked. He asked: 'How are you getting on at the Tyrrell place?'

'Alright. It's not pretty but it's comfortable at least.'

'Met anyone yet?'

'Only Mrs Payne who does for me, and the Dellers – do you know them?'

'Who doesn't? Amazing people – but extremely nice.'

'I'm glad you think so. I must say they couldn't have

been kinder or more hospitable and I imagine I'm not really their cup of tea.'

'I don't think they're the least critical – or he's not at any rate. He likes his grog, but he's one of the straightest men I've ever come across. And he throws his money about – there's no cause too small for him to support, he's a real soft touch. I don't think he's specially religious, they come to church at Christmas, yet he gives most generously to any charity, both cash and time – he even hauls chairs around the town hall for the WI.'

'He must be popular.'

'Oddly enough, not really. The village people are funny, they don't like to feel patronised. I suppose they think they're being softened up. They resent his wealth, his foreignness.'

'I suppose I see that. It seems perverse though!'

'Well there are other things too. The Dellers' girl, Susan – did you meet her?'

'Yes.'

'Fascinating, isn't she?'

'I thought so.'

'They don't. They're suspicious. She doesn't add up to their picture of what a young girl should be.'

'She is strange.'

'Yes, there is something, though I don't know what. The parents are rather defensive, it seems to me, though they obviously adore her.'

We walked a little way in silence. I liked Thorne, though I wasn't sure whether he was the ideal spiritual leader for a small country parish. He had a gossipy openness which was distinctly unclerical. It was obvious from the number of greetings he exchanged during our progress up the street that he was popular. I asked: 'How's your congregation here?'

He pulled a face. 'They're a heathen lot. They respect the

church, they want it to be there, they like to see me with my collar back to front, but as for turning up on Sunday . . .' He shook his head. 'The old people do, and I have a thriving Sunday school but the rest are tares and stony ground. Forgive my asking –' he shot me a penetrating glance – 'but shall I see you on Sunday?'

'I can't pretend to be a regular church-goer.'

'I didn't ask that.'

'Well –' I laughed at his directness – 'since this is meant to be something of a new start for me, I'll come, yes.'

'Thank you.' He slapped me on the shoulder. 'Here you are.'

We stopped outside the Lamb and Flag. I suddenly thought of something.

'I'd like to talk to you some time – only local gossip.'

'Doesn't sound like a job for a man of the cloth.' He was laughing. 'But I know what you mean – the vicarage has replaced the barber shop as the centre of communications. I am, however, a respecter of privacy.'

'Oh, it's nothing sensitive.'

'How much time do you have now?'

I glanced at my watch. It was only just midday. 'Plenty.'

'Well, I have to see the verger in church in about a quarter of an hour. Wait while I nip in here –' he indicated a greengrocers – 'and walk down with me.'

When he re-emerged with a string bag full of apples and sprouts he explained, half-apologetically, 'My wife has almost more duties than me, hence the shopping.'

We crossed the road and began to move down the other side.

'What's your question then?'

'Deller mentioned a girl who disappeared –'

'Marion Dukes – about four years ago.'

'I just wondered what you knew about that. Missing

without trace, and so on – it must affect a small place like this.'

'Oh yes, beyond doubt it does.'

'I gather they suspect the chap who works in Deller's garden.'

'Jan Holz? Yes, I wondered if you'd heard about that. Of course, that's another reason they dislike Deller himself. I believe his employing the man was intended as a genuinely charitable gesture but they see it as flying in the face of local opinion.'

'And what do you think of him – the German, I mean?'

'It's almost impossible to have an opinion, he's such a lone wolf. He's devout – one of my sidesmen, as a matter of fact – but he doesn't say much. I suppose, if anything, I like him. Private sort of chap, he's put up with a lot of bad feeling without ever retaliating. He certainly had nothing to do with the child.'

'You think not?'

'No. It's rubbishy, vicious prejudice that hung that tag on him. Because they can't explain him, they accuse. Also, of course, he does like children, and is good with them . . .'

'Why are you so sure it wasn't him?'

'No facts, I'm afraid, simply that he's the sort of person who wouldn't *bother*, if you know what I mean. Control is high on his list of important qualities. Besides, if he had done it, I don't think for a moment he'd still be here living in the middle of all this gossip and suspicion. I'm surprised he puts up with it even so.'

'I see.'

'You don't really, do you?' Cyril Thorne smiled into my face. 'Not to worry. I expect all this prejudice seems barbaric to a Londoner like yourself.'

'A little, I must admit. It's so petty, and yet so vicious.'

'Petty? Yes, in some respects I suppose that's right. But

remember a child disappeared. Her parents were well-liked people. It made everyone in the village feel threatened.'

We had arrived at the lych-gate leading into the church. Cyril Thorne turned to me: 'Do you want to take a look at the church since you're here?'

'I'd like to.'

We strolled up the path to the main entrance. The church was perched on a small hill, the graveyard sloping away steeply behind it to where a rickety wooden fence separated it from a narrow field with some pigs. Straight ahead beyond the church, the open country stretched away. To our left were the blank side walls of the pebble-dash cottages of Ballacombe. The graves were like so many silent people standing on the well-kept grass – there was an old man weeding laboriously in one corner – and they seemed to speak of their occupants. Baroque Victorian monoliths jutted sternly over small, moss-covered stones, the memories of children from a less fortunate age. Shiny marble crosses spoke eloquently of the deceased's prosperity, and little tile-edged plots with no stone at all were marked only by jam pots full of buttercups. The wind snaked and slithered among them. The old man looked up and touched his cap to Cyril Thorne. The priest's wisps of grey hair fluttered in the breeze.

Inside the church the twilit silence and stillness struck as heavy as a blow after Nature's movement outside. Cyril Thorne said: 'I have to see to one or two things, I'll leave you now – but do come on Sunday.' We shook hands and he strode off up one of the side aisles, his crêpe rubber soles squelching on the flagged floor.

There is something compelling about a church, even to someone like me who hardly ever steps into one except out of curiosity. Now I wandered slowly round the edge of the nave, reading the plaques on the walls, fingering the hymn books, peering through the carved screen behind the font at the bell-rope hanging like a hangman's noose in the dark of the belfry. Someone had done the flowers over a week ago, I guessed, for the edges of the Michaelmas daisies were brown and curled, and the greenery as crisp and brittle as paper. Occasionally a leaf dropped on to the stone floor with a sound tiny as a pinprick. The walls were thick with plaques and commemorative stones, from huge slabs of verbose verse, with stanza after stanza of fulsome and humourless panegyric, to tiny squares, with no more than a name carved on one of the slabs of stone that made up the wall. A great many of the names that appeared on the gravestones were here too. The words returned my curious gaze fixedly – stern, immutable, accusing, like the sightless watching eyes in a waxworks. It was so quiet I seemed to hear the last breaths of the dying flowers. I wondered where Cyril Thorne had gone. I came full circle, and looked through the arched tracery of the rood screen – it reminded me of Deller's meticulous rose trellis – at the altar, plain and still covered with a white cloth. I thought: Everything I see now was probably just like this a couple of hundred years ago – nothing's changed. Everything around me at the moment was, is, will be, like this. Quite suddenly something made me turn. A small figure was standing against the light that sifted in at the door of the church – the shoulders were hunched, the head slightly to one side, peering, questioning. Foolishly, the hair on my neck rose.

'Sorry, sir.' The voice was as wispy as a thread in the hollow silence, tailing away, as the little old man – the one we had seen in the graveyard – turned to go back to his work. I made some foolish explanatory remark, already too late, the grin of relief spread all over my face. I was shaking like a leaf. Hurriedly I left the church.

The old man was sitting on a tarpaulin just to the right of the porch, munching a bread roll. He looked muddy, fleshy, homely, nothing like the wraith who had so recently appeared in the doorway. I asked him: 'Did the old church path come right up here?'

'Oh, yes, sir.' He struggled to his feet, blowing crumbs, dusting his front. 'Come thisaway.' I followed him round to the far side of the church, where the pigs snuffled in the dip below the gravestones. Beyond the pigs were a couple of rather tatty post-war prefabs, lovingly humanised with flowerbeds, strings of washing, TV aerials. I followed the old man's arthritis-bent finger. 'Over there, sir, it comes, down from that small wood –' it was the wood above Tyrrell's cottage, that Deller had showed me – 'over the common, 'tis a nice walk down there, sir. Then it joins the road, and you lose it, till you see this, the very end of it here.' He pointed at a narrow weaving track between the graves that came up from the pig field and petered out in the paved way that ran round the church.

'So the gate from the village street is fairly recent.'

The old man grinned, displaying a glossy set of NHS dentures. 'I s'ppose you could call it that, sir – hundred and fifty years! But this 'yere –' he indicated the little path – 'goes back to when this was just a meeting place, no church buildin' at all.'

'It's very interesting. Thank you.'

He stood there, grinning at me. Suddenly I realised what he wanted. As I slipped him the coins I said, 'Thank you, again,' and he nodded slyly as if we had entered into some highly confidential pact.

'If you see Mr Thorne before he leaves, thank him for me, would you, and tell him I'll see him on Sunday.'

'He's in the vestry.'

'I don't want to disturb him.'

The village pub was warm, comfortable and provided a good snack lunch, over which I read a newspaper, my first in three days, to remind me of other matters, people and places. But they seemed unreal and faraway and my thoughts wandered. As I was about to leave I felt a hearty clap on my shoulder and looked up to see Deller, obviously *en passant*, a large tissue-wrapped bottle beneath his arm.

'Just been stocking up on the electric soup,' he said loudly, his great laugh shaking us both.

'I haven't thanked you yet—' I began, but he flapped my protestations aside with a large red hand.

'Well, don't. Glad I saw you actually because there are a couple of things I wanted to say.'

'A drink?'

'No, thanks, I must be rushing. I forgot to mention to you that my man Holz does the Tyrrell garden, where you're staying, once a month, so don't be surprised if he turns up.' He saw my question before I uttered it. 'I admit I persuaded your friend to take him on – told him it was an act of charity.'

'It's OK by me whoever does the garden as long as it's not my responsibility.'

'Good lad. The other thing is that Marjorie wants you to come to dinner with us on Saturday night. God knows why, but she does. Can you make it?'

'Well – I'd be delighted. It's extraordinarily kind of you.'

'Not kind at all. As I say, we've got a couple of others coming and the wife seemed to think you were what was needed to make the party go.'

'Thank you. What time?'

'About eight.'

'I'll see you then. Thanks again.' Deller hastened out of the pub, waving his bottle in farewell. I finished my drink and went to the newsagents to pick up Mrs Payne, thinking to myself how odd it was that I, a stranger in the village, should be so torn between the pagan past and the flourishing bourgeois present in the shape of the Dellers. And again I felt like the spider at the centre of a web.

That evening, after Mrs Payne had gone, another curious thing happened. I was up in my room getting ready for bed, and had left the window overlooking Church Path uncurtained as usual – I didn't think there would be anyone to see in. I had taken to going to bed early, and at nine thirty it was still only on the shady side of twilight outside. On a whim I went to the window and leaned on the sill. I glanced up at the small wood at the top of the hill, now just a black outcrop, opaque as rock against the dove grey evening sky. I pictured the processions, the horses and carts, the women on foot with their skirts dragging through the damp grass, the children skipping and running alongside, the happy brides, the tight-closed wooden boxes . . . and as I stared and imagined I saw, quite distinctly, like a pale ribbon across the fallow meadow beneath the wood, the path – Church Path – where it had for years been submerged. I peered, squinting, but it was there clear as a painting from a child's fairy story book, winding down the hill towards Rook's Cottage. And from somewhere, nowhere, but close, quietly and intimately I heard someone call, 'Michael.'

I'm certain I heard that voice, and when I had heard it the path faded, and the twilight seemed to deepen and there was nothing to see but the smudgy fields, nor to hear but the slam of a car door outside the Lamb and Flag.

Probably it was nothing, just one more evidence of auto-suggestion. But I was determined to walk up to the wood next day and exorcise the winding way which came right past my door.

Seven

On Saturday, the day of the Dellers' dinner party, autumn crept into the air. It was, after all, the beginning of September, and though the days since that terrible rain had been bright, breezy and mild, the evenings were stealthily closing in and growing colder and the first few, sad leaves began to drift down, covering neat lawns in rustling pools of brown and clogging gutters while we tried to pretend that it was still summer. With the first intimations of autumn my feeling of involvement in the village and its surrounding countryside increased. The fact of the season changing while I was there seemed to commit me, in some way, to the place – I began to see what Elise had meant when she had said so sadly: 'It'll be winter when you come back.' The days would get shorter – already there was a greyness about the evenings, a feeling of shadows growing and sunlight being eased away, usurped, and in turn becoming pale and half-hearted.

In the morning I went for a walk. I decided not to follow up my ill-fated sortie of a few days ago but instead to go up the hill, across the fields to the wood at the top, to see what the view was like and also to see if I could trace, from the top, the uphill journey of the church path. Since my imaginings of the night before, the path's fascination for me had increased. I was at the time extremely suggestible, even vulnerable. I felt at the mercy of my sick and wayward fancy, compelled to follow and investigate every oddity that occurred to me. My fears and dreams had become reality, my real life blurred and distant. The image I had of the people in the field had grown clearer in my mind than when I'd first seen it, as though it had burned itself into my brain. Now I was sure that I had seen Holz's face clearly, and in detail – I could even see things that I had not noticed when I had met him, things which were more nuances of expression and mood than of physical appearance. I observed a certain anxiousness in those stern dark eyes, a tension in the stillness. There was some anomaly, a bitter-sweetness, even when I recalled that arm raised to stab.

As I started my walk it was misty – a sure sign of autumn – but by the time I climbed the gate into the field above Rook's Cottage I had risen above what still remained of it, evaporating in wraiths in the valley of Ballacombe like the dying smoke from a number of wood fires. A big, blurred, cream-coloured sun stood over the wood at the top of the hill, enlarged by its vaporous halo. The sky was a lowering dun colour, trying to brighten but still overcast. I was quite alone on the hillside.

I thought, as I had in the parish church, that my surroundings at this moment were probably little different from what they had been hundreds of years ago. The land was fallow, a rough pasture of lush grass, interwoven with long-legged weeds. The banks and hedgerows that bordered it were densely knotted and tangled with blackberries and a jungle of roots and branches so that it was hard to tell which was solid earth and which vegetation. I thought they must be full of small creatures pursuing their own ends, living their lives in that overgrown world – birds, mice, snakes, insects. I had an odd idea that they might all be watching me – millions of tiny eyes staring brightly in the sheltered leafy darkness. And from the wood, too, there might be observers, larger ones. I thought of the fox I had seen in my garden a few nights ago. Perhaps he was paying me back for being one up on him. Perhaps he was up there, soft-footed on the pine needles beneath the trees, watching.

I was about two-thirds of the way up the field and becoming breathless. Remembering how I had felt prior to my experiences on the first walk, I stopped, and turned, hands in pockets, to look back the way I had come.

To my astonishment I turned to see someone else only yards away, trudging and waving, trying to come abreast of me. It was Susan Deller. I experienced that unreasonable shock that comes from suddenly realising that you have not been alone when you thought you were. If I had been caught stealing, or talking to myself, I could not have been more discomforted. And I had been walking so hard, so fast, like a man with a fiend at his heels.

As a result of this inner turmoil I stood with my mouth gaping open as Susan came up to me. She wore the same clothes as when I had first met her, but her handsome bony face was bright with the effort of hurrying up the hill, and she looked more relaxed and animated.

'Hallo,' she said. 'I thought I'd never catch you up.'

I regained my tongue. 'Were you trying to?'

'Can't you tell?' She clapped one large hand to her breast and panted ostentatiously.

'I'm sorry, I didn't see you.'

'I cut up diagonally from the corner down there.' She indicated the corner farthest from Rook's Cottage. 'That's probably why.'

'Shall we press on regardless?' I said stupidly, facetiously, and she nodded with a funny little smile as if she knew how awkward I was.

After we had started walking together she added, conversationally, making an effort: 'Dad gave me a lift to town and I was walking back up Church Path and across

that plough. I can get right back to the end of our garden
this way.'

'I was just walking the hill. Because it's there.' She
smiled the little smile again. 'What can I see on the
other side?'

'It's a bit of a false crest, quite a plateau really. You'll
have to go through or round the little wood and then for
nearly a quarter of a mile before you can go down the
other side.'

'I wondered where the church path came from.'

'I've no idea.' She seemed uninterested, so I didn't
pursue the subject. We trudged in silence, she far less
breathless than I, till we got to the edge of the wood.
We stopped, and she said: 'I must go my ways. You're
coming to dinner tonight, aren't you?'

'Yes, that's right. I'm looking forward to it.'

She looked as though she might have spoken but set
her lips firmly together and nodded instead. Her face
seemed shadowed again, something had slipped across
behind the eyes giving it that defensive closed look that
I first remembered. But she remained polite.

'I'll see you then.' She held out her hand, straight and
mannishly, and we shook. I thought, How odd, but at the
same time I noticed again how beautiful she was. So big
and strong and handsome, her skin clear and unmade up, her
impossibly unstyled hair thick, straight and shiny, asking
to be touched. In fact her appeal was that of a fit, strong
animal – no affectations, no additions or improvements, the
sort of natural good looks which are almost embarrassing
in a sophisticated urban setting but which seemed right
here against the black pungent columns of the pines. For
a moment I ached to be her friend, to solve or at least to
know her secret, to appreciate her mystery from the inside
instead of being, as I was now, cut off by it.

As she took her hand from her pocket a small brown

object fell to the grass and I stooped to return it to her.

'What's this?' I turned it in my hand, It was a small, beautiful wood-carving of an otter. Very simple, no sharp edges or intricacy, the sleek swimming shape of the animal merely suggested, the natural grainy shape and swirl of the wood left to tell its own story. It felt warm and smooth, almost animated as if the hands which had worked on it so lovingly had actually imparted life. 'It's beautiful,' I said, handing it to her.

'Thank you.'

'You didn't do it yourself?'

'Oh, good heavens no. As a matter of fact, it's what I've been to collect in the village.'

'You bought it? Where?'

'No, I didn't buy it . . .' She seemed suddenly different. Then I had the impression she took a deep breath, a hold on herself. 'Jan Holz makes them,' she said. 'He gave it to me, as a matter of fact.'

'Oh. Well I think it's superb – real craftsmanship.' I avoided the issue which she had so valiantly raised by implication. The carving went back into her pocket and she laced her big hands together awkwardly.

'Well,' I said. 'It was nice seeing you – and we'll meet again this evening.'

'Yes. Good-bye.'

'Good-bye for now.' I watched her as she turned and trudged away with long strides along the south edge of the copse, round its furthermost tip and out of sight. From the back she might have been some tall young farmhand, with the collar of her drab mac turned to hide her bobbing hair, and her cord trousers shoved bulkily into the grubby cuffs of Wellington boots. Her hands were plunged into her pockets and I guessed that the left one was curled lovingly round the little otter. When she eventually disappeared I experienced an almost physical wrench, a stunning sense of disappointment and loss, particularly as I knew she had taken her prized privacy in both hands and almost sacrificed it for my benefit. And I, too cowardly, or too embarrassed, or both, had pretended not to notice. Perhaps I'd never have another chance.

The wood, now that I was right at its edge, seemed bigger and more obdurate than I had imagined. Instead of a silent carpet of pine needles, its floor was a prickly and forbidding tangle of brambles and bracken with no immediately visible path through it. I began to walk along beside it, in the opposite direction to that which Susan had taken, looking out for a way through. About two-thirds of the way along I came to a slight opening in the thicket, like the estuary of a river and I could see the merest thread or suggestion of a path, just a crease in the undergrowth, leading back from it. For some obscure reason I was determined to walk through the wood if it could be done, rather than round it, I felt that it would be cheating to circumnavigate. I turned into the wood, and had taken no more than a couple of paces when I spotted something whitish amidst the bracken on my left. I bent and parted the ferns and discovered one of those small white-painted signs that are used to mark footpaths. This one was stained and chipped and partly covered with moss, but I could read it. It said, 'Ballacombe Church Path'.

So this was it, I was actually following the church path, coming the same way through the wood as all those brides, and coffins and processions and priests had done over God knows how many years. I felt quite elated by my discovery, but the walking was far from easy. It was more like hacking through tropical jungle than walking over the English countryside. After about ten minutes I looked back and realised that I was still only about twenty yards from the edge of the wood. The distant day beyond the shadow of the trees looked unusually bright compared with the gloom where I stood. I felt utterly cut off. The tangled undergrowth clung to my legs up to the knees. I looked ahead again and could not even make out the suggestion of a path. But the wood can't be all that wide, I thought. I must come out on the other side soon. I pressed on, plunging and stamping on the brambles, getting covered with scratches and increasingly aware that my shoes were wet, and the damp was seeping through to my feet. I supposed that the ground hidden from the sun must be permanently sodden. I glanced up and was relieved to find that the trees were not, as I'd begun to imagine, hundreds of feet tall but of fairly average height, and sparse enough to allow a few patches of pale sky to glimmer down. I pressed on.

After about a quarter of an hour I was surprised to come across a sudden change in the character of the wood. I had been walking so furiously, expending so much effort on simply placing my feet that I had been almost in a trance. Then I noticed that the path had reappeared before me, and this time not just a thread among the brambles but a wide, grassy rutted cart track with the undergrowth at a respectful distance on either side. I heaved a sigh of relief and began to stride out, assuming that I would now be out of the trees in a few minutes. But I'd gone no more than a few paces when I began to hear voices, coming the other way, towards me, and this accompanied by that horrible ringing in the ears which I now only associated with one thing. I pressed my hands to my temples, trying physically to squeeze the sound from my head but it persisted high and penetrating, and the voices grew nearer. They were the voices of a mixed group of people. A man shouting, children laughing and calling, a low chatter of conversation, somebody crying in an odd wailing fashion. And there was something else, an uneven booming beneath the babel of voices. I recognised it as the creak and rumble of heavy wheels. The sounds got closer and closer until they literally enveloped me, though there was nothing to see but the grass, the bushes, the trees. I reeled and covered my head with my arms as the noise buffeted me, but it was soon past. The ringing in my head faded and I began to run as hard as I could, gasping and moaning for breath, till I burst out of the trees on to a stretch of open heath. Even then I continued running, my head up, my feet striking the ground like pistons.

When I was too tired to run further, almost a quarter of a mile from the wood, then and only then did I look back. The wood seemed to have closed behind me like a door. It appeared small, dark and secretive, the trees clustered like a tight knot of men in dark cloaks against the skyline. Not big enough, I thought, for what I had experienced, the tears of fright trickled down my cheeks as my breath sawed in and out of agonised lungs.

That afternoon I slept. I hadn't pursued my walk much further in the morning but had turned right and joined the road just below the Deller House, content to follow it home. When I'd got back I'd felt utterly exhausted. My confused and shocked brain had seemed to be functioning by instinct, quite separate from my body. It was an odd sensation, not unlike drunkenness: a heightened awareness accompanied by physical disability which made precise movements difficult. My hands had fumbled around, making a mess of heating soup and cutting bread, and I'd gulped a bit down but could taste nothing. I'd thought, I have no idea what I am doing here in this cottage. Why am I here in this strange house which belongs to someone else, what is going on around me, am I going mad? I'd left the kitchen littered with debris and went up to my room. The little bed looked plain and friendly, solid. I'd pulled back the counterpane, pushed my shoes off and curled up like a child with arms folded over my chest and my knees drawn up foetus-style. I just wanted to forget.

It was half-past six when I woke up and I remembered with horror that I had to go to the Dellers for dinner. I toyed with the idea of ringing and claiming illness, which was nearly true, but the thought of the long evening alone in the cottage appalled me and I went and ran myself a bath, telling myself that it would do me good to go out, make an effort, mix with ordinary people who didn't see ghosts. And yet not all so ordinary: I thought of Susan, and realised that I really *wanted* to see her, to make contact and perhaps make up the ground I had so feebly relinquished this morning. As I lay in the steaming water, I also determined to write to Elise. I had brushed her off but perhaps I needed her more than I cared to admit. Someone from my other life, someone to recall me to myself. And after all, God knows, she was my wife. Yes, I would write and ask her to come down for a few days. I would be positive, make moves, make decisions, push the horrors aside like the childish dreams they were.

It took me the best part of a quarter of an hour to get the Morris started. The little garage was cold and damp and the engine coughed wretchedly, refusing to fire. The familiar sound of its rasping and dying away reminded me again of winter. But I felt better now I was bathed, shaved and wearing a decent suit. The small, familiar rituals of self-preparation drove away any spooks, or least pushed them back into recesses at the back of my mind where they cast a vague shadow but not total darkness.

Deller House looked civilised and welcoming, lights blazing, and the front door standing open so that a flood of light poured out over the gravel drive. As soon as I drew up Arnold Deller appeared and ran down the steps to meet me. The impact of his large presence was therapeutic as on the first occasion when I had met him, only this time the whiff of whisky was a little stronger.

'Marvellous, marvellous,' he said, grabbing my hand in

his enormous palm and giving it a great tug of salutation. 'Come on in and have a drink. I can feel winter arriving out here this evening.'

I agreed that it was colder, and only too willingly allowed myself to be swept along, cosseted and cared for by this genial hospitable man. He closed the front door after us and led me into the sitting room, his fingers encircling my upper arm as though I were a child. It was obvious that I was the last to arrive. The other people in the room, aside from Marjorie and Susan Deller, were one man and one woman. The man was youngish, perhaps thirty, slim and I supposed good-looking in a slightly prissy way, with carefully styled dark hair and a slim figure nattily turned out in a cream suit and striped waistcoat.

'This is Ambrose Austen, a young journalist friend of ours,' said Arnold and the young man raised his glass to me. 'Cheers.' The woman was older, perhaps a bit younger than Marjorie but coarser, and more flamboyantly turned out. Her golden hair was piled in a teetering edifice of sausage curls on the crown of her head and she wore a low-cut pink dress with a glittering fringe just below the nipples which swung and bobbed as she talked. Her face was shining with sociability and heavily made up but her eyes were watchful and astute beneath their plucked brows. 'And this,' said Arnold, leaving me and putting his arm round the woman's thick and shiny waist as Marjorie slipped a glass into my hand, 'is our own, our very own Iris Evans. How shall I describe you, I?'

'Let's see.' Iris bridled and smiled at me. 'I think you could call me an old family friend . . .' This remark was greeted by gales of laughter.

Marjorie Deller, smiling but not, I noticed, laughing, said quietly to me by way of explanation: 'Iris used to live near us in Leeds – she used to go out with Arnold way back before he married me and when they're together they don't let me forget it.'

'Are you – both – staying down here?' I enquired generally. Iris made a face.

'I am, Mr Bowater, but only tonight. I'm on my way back from touring in Cornwall. I'd like to stay longer with dream boat here, but never mind.' More gales of laughter. Ambrose Austen came over to me, smiling in a man-to-man way, and stood with his back to the others.

'I'm staying,' he said.

'You're on holiday?'

'No, no, work.'

'Oh?'

'Yes, I'll tell you about it later. I'm here with these kind people over the weekend but then move out to the local hostelry for the duration. It's simpler – one can be wholly independent.'

'Of course.'

I wondered what in the world could bring a smart young journalist to a place like Ballacombe and would have asked him further, but my eye suddenly caught Susan's. She was sitting in a narrow upright wing chair in the far corner of the room, watching the proceedings in that silent, shut-off way of hers. I noticed she held a glass but it was full and untouched. She wore a red soft tweed dress, the colour of which was glorious but the style impossible – one of those long, semi-fitted tubular garments with three-quarter-length sleeves and a plain round neck. Her gangly legs looked awkward in sheer tights and her feet, in patent leather court shoes, were tucked under the chair, ankles crossed, as though they embarrassed her. I smiled and lifted my glass. Austen turned and followed my gaze.

'Old Suzie all on her own as usual,' he remarked, having nodded to her and turned back to me. 'It's time she was given a push.'

'Oh, do you think so?'

'Yes, I mean – you know her at all?'

'Slightly. I'm only a visitor here myself, so—'

'Well, it's ridiculous.'

He swigged the rest of his drink and reached for my glass with a questioning look, offering me another. I nodded. 'Thanks.'

Austen went to fetch the drinks, Marjorie scuttled by with an 'I must go and take a peep in the oven!' and I went over to where Susan sat. She looked up at my approach.

'Hallo,' I said, 'you look a bit isolated over here.'

'I'm quite happy.'

I believed her. 'Your mother's got a houseful tonight.'

'She likes it.'

'You don't.'

She gazed into her bitter lemon as though it were a crystal ball and smiled her tight little smile. She was incredibly ill at ease. I tried to think of something to say that would engage her interest. I could not, would not, be just one of the rest who were worlds away from her.

'I found where the church path goes through the wood this morning,' I observed, 'just after I met you.'

'Oh yes, there used to be a sign on the edge of the wood where it went in.'

'That's right, I discovered that – it was very overgrown but I spotted the white paint, what was left of it.'

'You didn't get through?'

'Yes – oh yes, I was quite intrepid.'

'You must have been. That wood's completely over-grown.' She looked up at me, and I thought, She doesn't believe me, she thinks I'm just a townie telling stories. Then she added: 'Still, the wood's very narrow, so I suppose . . .'

'It's not when you're backing through it, believe me,' I said, 'but it was worth it. I felt quite a sense of achievement.'

'Did you now?' It was Austen, back with drinks. 'Hallo, Suzie.'

'Hallo.'

'What was so worthwhile?' he enquired, apparently undaunted by his chilly reception from Susan. I thought 'old sparring partners' but replied: 'Nothing of great interest. I was describing my walk this morning.'

Susan said: 'I'm sorry but that wood's very tiny, no more than a copse really. It can't have taken you that long unless you were walking in circles.'

'Well I may have wavered a bit. But in the middle of it the path opened right out and it was pretty straight from there on.'

'I see.' She was ending the conversation but it was plain she didn't believe me. And somewhere in the back of my mind something nagged at me. I remembered what it was – when I had looked back at the wood, after I had run so frantically from it in terror, it had looked closed. There was no path breaking out of it, and it had looked small. I was suddenly miserable with nerves. Had I then imagined not only those voices from who knows when, but also the path, so broad and green?

'OK, are you?' asked Austen.

'Thanks, yes. I was just thinking.'

'Ah.' What a pair of oddities he must think us. I could feel his sharp, rather sly grey eyes on Susan and me as he tossed back the rest of his gin and said: 'Come on, looks like eating time.'

Marjorie showed us into the dining room. It looked welcoming and wealthy, luxurious even, with a big shiny table beautifully laid with silver and thick white napkins, and lit by candles in chunky silver candlesticks. I sat on Marjorie's right, opposite Iris Evans, and next to Susan, while Austen sat on Arnold's right. The food, served by a plump Polish girl called Marika, was plain but delicious –

cooked by Marjorie. We had mushroom soup, which was thick and grey and aromatic – none of that pale synthetic brew – then roast saddle of lamb with onion sauce, roast potatoes and a towering pile of tiny, crisp buttered sprouts; and finally a stupendous home-made ice cream, as rich and golden and craggy as butter. It was an honest, delicious, sustaining meal, without frills or pretensions but redolent of the kindness and hospitality of our hosts. I thought of the number of dinners I'd been to with Elise in London where we had sat through five courses, all of them miniscule and so highly flavoured that they cancelled each other out. This was a meal to look back on.

Conversation remained fairly general until the eating was finished. Arnold produced a decanter of tawny port and passed it round. Marjorie said: 'If anyone wants the bathroom they know where it is, but I like a glass of port, and I'm not retiring.'

'And I'm not the retiring type!' added Iris, with a shriek of laughter, but added: 'But I will go and powder my nose. Save some for me, dear,' she said, tapping Arnold on the shoulder.

'Some what?' he threw after her roguishly as she left, and we heard her delighted cackle of laughter fade up the stairs. I glanced at Marjorie to see how she took all this trying badinage, but she looked calm and cheerful. It was not a situation I could see going down well where I came from, and I admired her for her sophistication. She must either be very sure of her man or very sure of herself.

Sipping my port, I asked Austen: 'Can I ask you now what you're doing down here?'

'By all means.' He tilted his chair back with a Cheshire cat smile and as his jacket fell back from the striped waistcoat, I saw a gold chain strung across it. I was becoming more and more certain that I didn't like him. 'I'm doing a series for one of the Sunday supplements.'

'What on? Backwaters of rural England?' It was Marjorie, and I realised that even my hosts were not as yet aware of what their guest was working on.

'By no means,' said Austen. 'Far more spicy. The series is about unsolved crimes and I'm in Ballacombe to do some nosey-parkering about the disappearance of Marion Dukes.'

'How exciting!' It was Iris Evans, returning newly pinked and powdered from upstairs. 'Are you going to turn up new evidence?'

'Who knows? I might, but I somehow doubt it. Of course it would be a feather in my cap if I did.'

Susan, who had been quiet all through the meal, pushed her chair back and said softly: 'Excuse me, I think I'll go and see how Marika's doing.'

'Oh, don't do that, dear!' It was Iris again, catching Susan's hand as she passed. 'She's paid for the job. Stay and talk.' I saw the oddest look on Susan's face as she hesitated, then came back to her chair with a murmured 'I just thought I might help.' It was only there for a second, as her eyes met Iris's. There was a softness, the defences were down for a second. And then she had given in. I thought it odd that this rather vulgar, insensitive woman should so easily dissuade Susan, who obviously found the turn in conversation distasteful. But dissuade her she had, and Susan sat stern and silent next to me, her hands curled into fists, fingers down, on her lap, staring at her wrists. Her face was hidden from me by the falling curtains of her black hair and I ached for her lack of *savoir-faire*. She was like an embarrassed, discomforted child forced to remain in the company of adults when she wanted only to escape. I looked up to see Iris Evans's eyes also resting on her and there was something in her look – something smug and appraising, which annoyed me.

Austen was talking away: '. . . of course I've already seen the Dukes people – they moved to North Devon, and I went to Barnstaple first to speak to them.'

'Did you discover anything?' asked Arnold. 'I should think they find it hard to talk about, don't they?'

'Oh, it's a few years ago now, they're used to answering questions. Too used, probably, they sound as if they're speaking lines. They can't look at the thing freshly.'

'What sort of girl was she?' I asked, less because I wanted to know than to prevent Susan being dragged into the discussion.

'Well, you know how it is with mums and dads – they described her as a bright and cheerful girl, lots of friends, no trouble, full of life, etcetera ad nauseam.'

'It could be true.' His flippancy aggravated me.

'It could be, and I think it's just one side of the coin. Sure she was bright and cheerful – it's my opinion she was a sharp little flirt as well, and when she was out there being "no trouble" she was teaching the local secondary school lads a thing or two. I'm certain that whatever she got she asked for it.'

'That's a wicked thing to say.' It was Susan.

'You think so, do you, Suzie?' said Austen patronisingly, letting his chair tip forward again and leaning on the table, grinning at her.

'Yes.' Susan met his eyes, blushing hard, her face grim. 'And it's not true. I knew her.'

'Oh, hardly, dear,' Marjorie's voice held a note of maternal warning. 'Surely.'

'Well I did . . .' Susan looked down at her fists again. 'I met her a few times. She was nice. Fun, full of life. I liked her.'

'Well, good for you,' said Austen. 'I've nothing against the girl myself. But I'm here to tell you that she played a dangerous game.'

113

'She was only thirteen.' Marjorie was making light of it, and I was glad.

But Iris Evans quite gleefully came down on Austen's side. 'Oh, Marge, you're too soft. Girls of thirteen can be kids or they can be women. And country girls are often more advanced than town girls. They watch the animals . . .' She giggled at her own humour, but even Arnold didn't join her.

Instead he remarked: 'You'll stir up a lot of feeling, lad. You know who suspect number one is, don't you?'

'No.' I could see Austen's ears prick up.

'My gardener, Jan Holz.'

'Polish?'

'German, ex POW.'

'Probably just prejudice.'

'I'm relieved to hear you take that line, Ambrose – I adhere to it myself. He's straight and a good worker and there's absolutely no proof against him, no evidence even. If there's one thing I hate it's witch hunts.'

'On the other hand . . .' said Austen – and I thought 'meddler' – 'there's no smoke without fire.' He looked dapper and smug, glancing round at our faces, pleased with his small quota of power. 'I mean, a bit of an outcast and so forth. He might have fancied a little revenge on village society.'

'You surely don't believe that.' It was Susan again. 'And anyway you've never even met him.' Her voice was tight and her face pinched, she was angry.

'Don't worry, Suzie, old girl, I'm not about to pillory the chap, it's just that one should keep an open mind.'

'Oh.'

There was a brief silence broken by Marjorie's 'Let's go in the other room, shall we?'

Fortunately for us all conversation after dinner was kept general. Perhaps all of us had sensed that we were on quaking ground with the subject of Marion Dukes, and Jan Holz's possible guilt. Ambrose Austen, the Dellers and I discussed housing in general and urban housing in particular (about which I knew nothing but Austen appeared a fund of information) and Iris Evans and Susan sat together on the sofa deep in conversation. At least, Iris appeared to do most of the talking, but as far as I could make out Susan seemed not simply content, but positively eager to listen, with many smiles and nods. I couldn't for the life of me see what she found attractive in the woman. She seemed the very last person to appeal to the Susan I recognised – so reserved, so special, so 'other'.

I left fairly early – about eleven thirty – partly because I was tired but mainly because the evening had turned sour on me. It wasn't easy to say why – certainly not merely because of my dislike of Ambrose Austen and the job he was doing. Somehow my picture of people had been jiggled and shaken so that it no longer made a harmonious whole.

It was Susan, Susan . . . I realised that her image preyed on my mind more of the time than I'd previously cared to admit. Why did she like Iris Evans? I felt – jealous? Surely not, but when I thought of that woman's face, her make-up, her golden edifice of hair, her well-upholstered curves, I bristled with irritation. Thank God, I thought, she would be gone tomorrow. But even her departure wouldn't solve the mystery of her attraction for Susan Deller.

That night the cottage seemed bleak and grey and in the small hours, as I lay wide awake staring at the parchment lightshade on the ceiling, it began to rain again.

Eight

The following morning I woke late but with the feeling that I had hardly slept. I had dreamed a lot, a weird tapestry of faces and places, familiar yet unrecognisable, turning, looking, disappearing. I couldn't remember what, if any, the train of events in my dream had been, but I retained a strong impression that people had been eluding me, that I had been searching, running, catching up with my quarry only to have him or her brush past my fingertips and away at the last moment. As I sat over my coffee and cornflakes in the kitchen, there was a shadow over me, like one of those bruises of which you can't recall the cause.

Mid-morning, I rang the Dellers to thank them for the dinner party, but only Marika was there and I doubted whether she reeled in enough of my message to pass it on. I wondered where the family could be on a Sunday morning, since I knew from the horse's mouth that they weren't church-goers. Then I remembered that someone had said they might go part of the way back with Iris Evans, lunching at a hotel in Dorset, and assumed that this plan had been put into effect. Then, as I washed up my things I remembered my promise to Cyril Thorne. It was too late to get to matins now but I could go and make my apologies when the service was over – it was a pleasant walk, would give me something to do. Having decided, I felt more cheerful and thought that, in addition, I would write a note to Elise asking her down for a few days – I could post it in the village. She had been on my conscience more than somewhat since our telephone conversation. I knew I had been irrational and boorish and, who knows, it might do us both a bit of good to get together again for a while. I could not even remember what reason I'd given for her not coming down, she must think me quite imbalanced. I dressed hurriedly and perched on the side of my bed to write the letter. On a piece of narrow-rule manuscript paper I scribbled:

Dear Elise,

On mature reflection I realise how oddly (and rudely) I behaved when we spoke the other evening. The fact is I *have* been in a strange frame of mind, unable to marshal my thoughts, a good many bad dreams etc. and I can only offer these circumstances as an excuse. Please forgive, darling, and why not come down for a few days? That would be better than my coming to town as I feel the benefits to be gained down here are cumulative, so better to stick with it. Also it would do you good to have a break, and see how the other half lives. It's pleasant here, muddy and hilly, it will bring roses to your cheeks and bore you to tears. Just give me a ring to say when you want to come – the middle of this week?

All my love,
Michael

I felt pleased with this effort, especially the touch about her being bored to tears – would get her down like a shot. We understood each other, I realised, even after all that had happened. I sealed the envelope, scribbled the familiar Hampstead address on the front and set out to walk down to the village.

It was soaking wet everywhere after the night's rain but

117

the sky was pale and light and the air mild. Real Devon weather, soggy and soft and enervating, the fat, round hills like so many sleeping pigs all around, the cottages closed and drowsy, even sounds – footsteps, birdsong, car engines – deadened by the damp lushness. Walking quickly, which I hoped would clear my head, was like wading through tepid water. The Sunday hush pervaded even a countryside that was habitually quiet. The sounds of tractors, of people walking, were gone. All was torpor and puddles.

I deliberately kept my mind as blank as I could as I retraced the steps I had taken on my first morning in Ballacombe. I counted my footsteps, sidestepped puddles scrupulously, collected some blackberries from the hedge and ate them from my cupped hand one by one. I came to the gate into the ploughed field and climbed over it. This was an exorcism. The complete non-reaction, the continued moist stillness, the squelch of the craggy red clay under my shoes drove away spectres like the sign of the cross. It was just a field, rows of furrows regular as telegraph wires curving away above the rise.

I made my way round the edge toward the corner where the gate to the church path was. The going was quite rough, for the plough was no good to walk on, and the margin between that and the hedgerow was narrow. The brambles and stiff twigs scratched the sleeve of my mac as I walked but the touch, it seemed to me, was friendly rather than menacing.

Once out of the field I enjoyed the experience of walking over new ground. I was now out on the heath land and the path was plain to see, two parallel threads of worn, stony earth stretching away. The sun was beginning to break through and it shone on the blond grass, which was tussocky and firm, springy as a mattress. I walked briskly – it was all downhill, my bugbear was behind me and the letter to Elise crackled in my pocket, feeding me with a warm glow of virtue.

It took about twenty minutes of brisk walking to come out on the corner where the main Ballacombe road curved into the village. I could hear the organ faintly from the church, and see people spilling out of the porch into the friendly lay sunshine, wearing blazers, pullovers, print frocks – a predictable congregation profile. Outside the porch I could see Cyril Thorne, rubicund and pristine in his surplice, shaking hands and exchanging pleasantries. The exodus was thinning to a trickle. I stood to one side and waited till the last worshipper had been processed, and then stepped forward.

'Mr Thorne.'

'Bowater, my dear chap, you made it!'

'Well – I didn't, I'm afraid. I woke too late, but I thought I should come down and let you know I'm not a complete ne'er-do-well.'

'I never thought any such thing, it's delightful to see you. How are you settling in?'

'Very well, I feel better today.'

'You've been feeling ill?'

'Not ill. Tired, confused, bit below par – that type of thing.'

'Ah. That type of thing. Say no more.' He gave me a penetrating look. In his full uniform he seemed slightly less approachable, more impressive. I almost wished I had attended his service. He said: 'Shall we walk in the direction of Glebe House?'

'Certainly, I've only got to post a letter, then I thought I'd have a beer at the pub and walk back.'

'I'd ask you in for a drink with us, but it so happens we have the curate and his wife from Ballacombe West coming to lunch, and since I have to be back for family communion at two I think I should put in a punctual appearance.'

119

'That's quite alright, it was kind of you to think of me.'

'Still concerning yourself with the village mystery?'

'Not intentionally. But everyone may have to quite soon.'

'Oh? Why so?' I explained briefly about the arrival of Ambrose Austen and its implications. As I finished, a tall dark figure in an old-fashioned double-breasted suit emerged from the vestry door to the side of the church and made off down the path. I remembered Thorne telling me that Jan Holz was a sidesman and immediately recognised the thin, straight figure. Cyril Thorne followed my gaze. 'Poor chap, in that case I'm afraid he's in for a time of it.'

'I should think so. Whether or not fresh suspicion is actually cast on him I imagine it will stir up all the old feelings.'

'Indeed it will. And not so old either. A lot of them are too close to the surface as it is.'

'Where does he live?'

'In a council bungalow unfortunately.'

'Unfortunately?'

'It doesn't do anything to improve the feeling against him. He got it fair and square, waited his turn, and he's a good tenant. The garden's a picture.'

'I can imagine.'

'I don't know. Damn journalists. I suppose they'll justify it to us by saying they may find the girl.'

'I didn't have the impression that Austen was over-bothered about justifying himself to anyone.'

'I just hope he keeps a sense of proportion about the whole thing. It simply is not worth disturbing several hundred lives and blighting a few more on the off-chance of finding a girl who is almost certainly dead, if not buried. Charity is for the living. The Dukes were sensible people, they've recovered, but heaven knows what the resuscitation of the case may do. It makes me very angry.'

I sensed that the vicar meant what he said, the round face above the snowy surplice was crimson. We had reached the gate of Glebe House. 'I'm sorry if I seem intolerant,' he said, in a way which sounded anything but contrite, 'but these things make my blood boil. It's meddling, destructive, thoughtlessly cruel. If this fellow comes to see me I shall tell him so.'

'I wish you would,' I said, and meant it. For I thought of Susan Deller, who had known Marion Dukes – another of her stranger, ill-starred, ill-chosen friendships, and who, God knows, could not be more vulnerable to the pryings and baitings of a man like Austen. She had no tact, no caution, no protective carapace of discretion.

We parted and I made my way to the Lamb and Flag, posting my letter to Elise on the way up the hill.

Business was booming. The public bar was packed with non-churchgoers, whose high colour and general jollity proclaimed their presence there for some time. The saloon bar, into which I tentatively stepped, was almost as full, but mostly with members of the congregation and a few of the jollier wives, having a before-lunch tipple, and a few hardy perennials sitting at stools at one end of the bar. I was strongly conscious of the village *en masse*, all its factions represented, a cohesive whole instead of a scattering of subjective impressions. I felt shy and out of place. I spotted Mrs Payne and Len sitting on a bench seat, she with a snowball, he with a stout, accompanied by two friends; all were dressed up. I caught Mrs Payne's eye and she nodded, tight lipped, lifting her glass a little but I sensed that this was not the time to engage her in conversation.

Like a nervous schoolboy I made my way to the bar and ordered a light ale. As I was taking my first delicious sip from the frothy surface I felt a touch on my shoulder and a voice said: 'We both seem to be boozing alone.'

I turned. It was Ambrose Austen, Scotch in hand, as dapper and unctuous as ever.

'Oh, hallo,' I said, my conversation with Cyril Thorne still too fresh in my mind to bother to disguise my lack of enthusiasm. He raised his eyebrows.

'Sorry for living.'

I realised I had been rude. After all, the man had done nothing yet, as far as I knew.

'I'm sorry, did I sound short?'

'A little. No matter. Let's breathe a bit, shall we?' We emerged from the crush of the bar.

By way of conversation and also because I genuinely burned to know, I asked: 'Made any enquiries yet?'

'Not actually. I've been attending to my domestic arrangements – I've moved down here now, you see.'

'Here? This pub?'

'The same. They have four rooms, B. and B., and very nice too.'

'I'm surprised you didn't stay on with the Dellers.'

'You shouldn't be. It's much better to be one's own boss, so to speak, not to have any ties. After all, who knows what may come up?'

I looked up at him, but his face gave away nothing. It was a neat little face, as smooth and unreadable as a waxwork.

'Whatever do you mean?'

'What I say. It's better not to be under obligations. That's all . . .' He flashed me his bright, cold smile. 'Have another.'

Since he had already taken the glass from my hand I was left with no alternative but to stand and aimlessly wait for him. He was the sort of person, I realised, who entirely sapped my initiative, so that, although I disliked him, he remained always one step ahead of me, brisk and unruffled, while I trailed irritably in his wake, longing to voice my objections but never quite making it.

As I stood there, gazing round me at the surging throng of Ballacombe locals enjoying their Sunday pint I noticed the merest cat's-paw of shock, saw faces turn, eyes stare, conversations flag almost imperceptibly, before it picked up again, glasses were raised and the status quo – or was it? – was resumed. Jan Holz had entered the public bar.

You hear of prejudice, of a community's hackles rising for no good reason other than an imagined tribal suspicion, but I had never encountered it till then and it was as nauseating as a blow in the solar plexus. He'd come in very quietly, letting the door swing silently shut behind him, but his very quietness conveyed an impression of stealth, so that although they could not have heard him everyone was aware of his arrival.

He moved through the mass of people, his face impassive, swinging his shoulders to slide between men who would not move out of his way, barely brushing anyone, appallingly careful. At the bar the girl was fractionally slow to serve him, her fat country face black with mulish hostility. I watched Holz's hands – long and, though callused, fine – pass over the change and his strong fingers clasp the tumbler of beer. I thought, looking at those hands, that the good folk of Ballacombe were playing with fire when they ostracized Jan Holz. He gave an impression of enormous strength, both moral and physical, kept under iron control, and a calm that was part disdain, part reticence. One day something – or somebody – was going to rupture that calm. I thought of what I had 'seen' in the ploughed field. Perhaps that was it, I'd seen the moment of truth. But against whom? I couldn't picture Holz bothering to turn so violently on any of these stolid, narrow-minded country colonels or shopkeepers. No, it had to be someone who caused a spark.

Had I been able to go on thinking along these lines, I might well have reached the conclusion which was finally, and bitterly, forced on me. But as it was, I felt a nudge to my elbow and found Austen back, a glass in either hand. He passed me mine and followed the direction of my eyes. 'Aha,' he said in his smug way. 'The cat who walks by himself.'

Holz was standing very upright and alone amongst the crush of people at the public bar, as though the business of sipping his ale demanded complete concentration.

I said: 'Did you feel that hostility when he came in?'

'Indeed. They're small-minded people.'

'Oh?' I was surprised, not because I didn't agree, but because I hadn't expected Austen to hold that view.

However, he went on. 'But one should never underestimate the power of prejudice.'

'I don't think I do.'

'I mean that it can create what it suspects where there was nothing before.'

'You're telling me that prejudice can literally bring on the very thing it thinks it condemns?'

'Exactly that.'

'No . . .' I shook my head.

'Why not?' Prejudice is an isolating factor. When you ostracise someone you make them bitter and resentful. They are then surely likely to behave in precisely the way you originally foretold.'

'Well . . .' I was forced to admit that there was a certain grim logic in what he said. We both looked again at Holz, who was draining his glass preparatory to leaving. To our surprise he then made off not in the direction of the main door of the public bar, but to the side, out of our view, and presently appeared in the saloon bar, through the adjoining door. His arrival on the scene here was not greeted with so marked a reaction: for one thing we had already seen him come into the pub and for another the rather more gin-and-tonic set in this half had the manners to suppress their mutterings and confine themselves to a few raised eyebrows. To my amazement – I could not see Austen, for he stood slightly behind me – Holz kept on coming and only stopped when he stood in front of us. His handsome, melancholy face was as closed and secretive as a sealed letter: the message was there, hidden but waiting. When he spoke, his voice was as soft and even as it had been on our first encounter and yet it carried clearly through the babel of bibulous small talk.

'Good morning, Mr Bowater.'

'Good morning to you. Can I buy you a drink?'

'No, thank you, I am about to go. It was your companion –' his eyes flicked beyond me to Austen – 'I wished to speak to.'

With grateful relief, for somehow I was discomforted and guilty, I stepped aside. Austen was smiling questioningly but his eyes were cold. I thought, these two men are natural enemies, they loathe each other, they exist to prey on one another. And then, quickly, frighteningly: The natural law will assert itself.

Holz said softly: 'I hope you are not going to make people unhappy, Mr Austen.'

'So do I.'

'You will try? Or will you simply write your article with blood.'

This melodramatic phrase, uttered in that gentle, well-modulated voice chilled me to the marrow. It was shocking, but Austen threw back his head and laughed.

'My dear chap, you're coming on a little strong, aren't you?'

'I'm afraid – for many people.'

'Yourself among them, I have no doubt,' snapped Austen sharply as though, having indulged a fanciful child, he now had no further time to waste. 'For God's sake don't let your imagination run away with you. I'm a professional journalist. I shall do my job here and then get back to town as soon as I can – the rural backwaters of the west country are not my scene, nor am I even especially interested in this story. But as I say, I'll do the job in the way I know how.'

Holz did not reply. One or two of the people standing nearest us had stopped talking and were looking on with interest. But the German remained silent, nodded once, in a kind of fatalistic agreement, and left.

'Christ,' said Austen, 'it's me for the other half. You?'

I shook my head. 'I think I'll be going.'

'Embarrassed, were you?'

'I was, a little. He has a disturbing manner.'

'Apparently I have the same effect on him, if it's any comfort to you.'

'Oddly enough, I didn't get the impression he was especially bothered by you.' I took considerable satisfaction in saying it, and it was true. 'In fact I felt that the whole episode was something in the nature of a warning.'

'Warning? He was shit scared.'

'That's not true, and you know it.'

'I don't. I disagree. That is fact. You're entitled to your opinion but don't try and tell me what I think. The man was scared, and scared people are aggressive.'

Yes, I thought. They are.

'Listen,' said Austen, tapping my chest with his empty glass, 'your trouble is you reject the obvious. Who's the loner around here? Who's the popular suspect, the outcast, the whipping boy? Herr Holz, that's who. And he knows bloody well that I may get too close to the truth for his comfort.'

126

'But you don't know what the truth *is*, you're simply playing along with popular prejudice.'

'There's no smoke.'

I looked at his eyes again, cold and uncaring above the unctuous little mouth. 'You're out to get him,' I said.

'Who, me?'

'You can't afford to be flippant.'

'Alright then. Seriously, I don't like him.'

'You should be careful.'

'Don't tell me what I should be, there's a good chap.'

We looked at each other, he irritable, I frustrated and anxious. 'Well –' he made a pretence of draining his already long-empty glass – 'if you're not going to join me in another I'll say cheerio.' And he went off towards the bar.

I left. Outside it was turning into a fine afternoon, wet roofs and puddles glistened in the pale sunshine. After the intimate, boozy burble of the pub it was utterly still in the village street as I made my way down the hill. Obviously the non-drinkers among Ballacombe's population were tucking into their roast joint and two veg. I glanced at Glebe House as I went by. It looked solid, comforting and comfortable. I felt sure Mrs Thorne cooked an excellent leg of lamb. I had a sudden nostalgic, powerful longing for the comforts of home, a glass of good sherry, the smell of gravy, apple crumble, the Sunday papers. And I realised at the same time that my nostalgia was allied to my host of ever-present fears.

Something in the back of my mind was edging forward, trying to make itself known as I considered the antipathy between Holz and Ambrose Austen. Natural enemies, mutual predators placed in a situation where there could only be conflict. And the natural law . . . what happened when two enemies met in the animal world? The animal with territorial authority drove off the invader, the basic rule gave him the strength he needed. Suddenly it was there, bright, clear and startling in my mind's eye. Holz had met his victim. He was going to kill Ambrose Austen.

Nine

On Tuesday I received a letter from Elise.

Dear Michael

Of course I'll come down, I shall enjoy being muddy and bored, for a short while anyway. Could you meet my train in Exeter on Wednesday? It gets in at 12.30.

I decided to write to you for the same reason that I suspect you wrote to me instead of phoning – it's easier to stick to the point and avoid muddles. Shall we talk when we see each other?

Love, Elise

Holding her letter in my hand – tastefully thick white paper with spidery black writing – I went through to the kitchen where Mrs Payne was munching a biscuit and nursing a cup of weak tea at the table. It might have been gall and wormwood from the expression on her face. She glanced up at me, as she always did with that sharp, bird-like look of suspicion. I instantly felt that what I was about to ask would be an imposition.

'Mrs Payne – my wife would rather like to come down for a few days, would that be alright with you?'

'Of course. It's nothing to do with me, anyway.' She said this in a way that implied that she found the whole project a nuisance but would forbear to say anything.

'She's hoping to come down tomorrow,' I ventured, making it sound as though Elise's final decision depended entirely on the good will of Mrs Payne when I knew in fact that nothing would stop her at this stage.

'Very well, I'll make up another bed,' said Mrs Payne. It occurred to me that this would inevitably be in another room since Tyrrell's cottage was designed for bachelor living.

I decided to plunge in: 'Is there a double room in the cottage?'

'No, I'm afraid there isn't.' The 'I'm afraid' was a sure sign of her disapproval of, and mounting irritation with, the entire scheme.

'Oh. OK then. Yes, if you would be so kind.'

'I'll do it today.'

'That's very good of you. And by the way –' I had a sudden brilliant idea to ameliorate the inconvenience of Elise's arrival – 'Don't worry about the groceries and things while my wife is here, we'll manage.'

'I don't want to leave you a lot of work,' said La Payne, not without a touch of sarcasm.

'Not at all, you won't. It's been extremely good of you to do it at all, but we can certainly manage for the time being. If you could just come on your usual days to clean round a bit, you know –'

'Of course.'

'My wife won't be staying long. She has to get back to town.'

'That's alright.'

I slunk out, chastened by the confrontation and trying to picture in my mind's eye the spectacle of Elise conversing with Mrs Payne over the washing up. It was too hard – I gave up.

The prospect of Elise's imminent arrival served at least to turn my thoughts to more practical matters and while

Mrs Payne busied herself with the stairs, bedroom and bathroom I encamped in the sitting room and attempted to do some work.

As before, my concentration was poor. The quiet and aloneness which in the bustle of the city would have been ideal for the exercise of the intellect, here simply served to release my imagination so that I was continually seeing what I least wanted to – the image of Holz murdering Austen, who, I had now convinced myself, was his intended victim.

I also realised, with more curiosity than shock, that I was beginning to regard my dream, hallucination or whatever, as a reliable form of information, referring to it as one would to a photograph, identifying other characters and events from it. From seeing myself as the wretched victim of a nervous disorder I had somehow come to see myself as the holder of confidential information which invested me with superiority over others. By the same token I felt burdened by a sense of responsibility: since no one else could have experienced what I had, nor even be expected to believe that I had done so (I hadn't fully accepted it myself until lately), the burden of unravelling the implications and of preventing such an occurrence fell upon me. Perhaps the role of sleuth that I took upon myself was laughable, but I was shaken enough to accept it. And all the time the picture of Holz, knife in hand, standing over his victim on the muddy plough, grew clearer in my mind.

As I sat staring unseeing at my file of notes, I was disturbed by a brisk rapping on the window behind me. I turned to see Susan Deller in the garden, peering into the relative darkness of the cottage, smiling when I waved and she focused on me. I indicated the side door into the kitchen and went through to let her in.

'I'm afraid I'm muddy,' she said as I opened it.

'Don't worry,' I said, but at that moment Mrs Payne

materialised in the kitchen, looking at once curious and disapproving, and I added: 'Perhaps you could leave the boots here as Mrs Payne's just cleaned. Would you like coffee?'

Susan shook her head, I sensed she was discomforted – as who wouldn't be? – by the presence of the older woman, and I took her through to the sitting room. She looked round at it with interest.

'It's the first time I've been in here.'

'Really? As you see, it's not exciting.'

'I suppose not. It's not what I expected. It looks unlived-in.'

'It is, largely, I've only come in here to work. But I admit I should have thought Mr Tyrrell would have used it more.'

'I've never met him.'

'He's a pleasant chap – jolly, likeable, gregarious. He knows your parents.'

'Oh, I know that.' There was the slightest hint of irony. 'They make friends easily.'

There was a pause. I motioned her to sit down, but she seemed not to notice. I couldn't imagine why she had called in on me like this. She seemed a little edgy, excited, or nervous.

'I came—'

'My wife—'

We had both started to speak at the same time, and burst out laughing.

'Go on,' she said.

'I was just about to say,' I went on, 'that my wife is coming down for a few days.' Even as I finished the sentence I wished it unsaid. Somehow my remark had stifled something in Susan. The excited light went out of her eyes, her customary defensive quiet fell like a pall.

'Is she?'

132

'I thought it would be nice . . . London in the autumn . . . you know.' I stopped dead and gazed down at the key pattern on the faded carpet. Then something occurred to me. 'What were you about to say, anyway?'

But if I'd hoped to restore Susan's previous mood, and to draw from her whatever it was she wanted to discuss, I failed. It was too late. She shrugged, and folded her arms awkwardly.

'I forget.'

'Did you call for any special reason? I mean –' I didn't want to appear prying – 'it's so nice to have an unexpected visitor down here. I'm not used to this rural solitude.'

She didn't smile, but shrugged again, hugging herself. She seemed acutely embarrassed, in the way that I had been when she had walked up behind me in the field above Rook's Cottage. Whatever had been in her mind, it had been very close to her heart. Now perhaps she was disturbed by how close she had been to disclosing it to a relative stranger. She could apparently find no more words, but stood there staring down at her feet, her long arms wrapped round her.

I said gently: 'I wish you'd have that coffee.'

'Sorry?' Her head snapped up as though she'd been roughly awakened from a deep sleep.

'You're sure about the coffee?'

'Oh. Yes, yes, I only just wandered by . . . I must be off.' She headed for the door with enormous strides like a frightened colt.

'Off where?'

She didn't hear. Except for brief farewells nothing else passed between us as I saw her out of the front door. Yet again I had the agonising sensation of having missed something, of having been within an ace of great discoveries, a momentous turning point – but of having fallen short through my own clumsiness and stupidity. I turned back from the door just in time to see Mrs Payne's head withdrawing swiftly over the landing banister.

After lunch Marjorie Deller rang.

'Mr Bowater? I hope I'm not disturbing you.'

'Not at all. I don't seem to be getting much done down here anyway.'

'Well you may think this interfering of me, but Susan mentioned that your wife was coming down to stay for a few days.'

'That's right, I'm meeting her train tomorrow.'

'Now look, my dear, I appreciate you and your wife want lots of time to be alone together and enjoy the country air, but I wondered if we could steal an hour or two from you to come and have a drink with us on Friday evening. You're to say if you'd rather not, but we'd love to meet her if you feel you could make it.'

Swiftly, I tried to assess Elise's reaction to such an invitation and decided that its novelty would appeal to her.

'We'd love to,' I said.

'That's wonderful!' said Marjorie, sounding as if she really meant it. 'Nothing formal, come as you are, round about six o'clock.'

'We'll look forward to it. Thank you so much. I'm afraid I owe you an unreasonable amount of hospitality.'

'You do no such thing. We ask you because we like you.' I believed her.

'See you on Friday.'

I hoped I had not let myself in for an awkward occasion. The Dellers, I knew, would be enchanted by Elise. Everyone always was. But Susan – what would Susan make of my wife, and vice versa? For some reason I dreaded being distanced even further from Susan by the introduction of Elise on to the scene.

A Dangerous Thing

On meeting the London train at Exeter next day my vague unease about this meeting was confirmed. Elise stepped on to the platform looking like a fashion plate and gazing about her with the slightly aloof, benign curiosity I knew so well. Like moths to a candle, porters were drawn to her side. I simply waited for her, and her entourage of helpers and pigskin luggage, to come to me and then sweep on to the Morris Minor, where she distributed handsome tips and charming, ladylike smiles to all concerned. I held the door for her, climbed into the driver's seat, and kissed her again, on a soft perfumed cheek as passive and accepting as a baby's.

'You look wonderful,' I said.

'Thank you for saying so. You – you don't look well.'

'I'm not really myself,' I replied, taking the view that it was better to admit a little and hope for no further questions than to protest that all was well and face further interrogation. Elise placed her hand against my cheek.

'If this is doing you no good you should come back to London, you know,' she said softly, kindly, like a parent. 'It's unhealthy to brood down here if you're getting no better.'

I placed my hand over hers and she at once withdrew it. I started up the car and muttered: 'I didn't say it was doing no good.'

We drove for a while in silence. I cast covert glances at Elise's outfit. It was new, and obviously represented some kind of concession to the rustic life she was about to sample. A chocolate-brown trouser suit in very fine wool over a cream silk shirt, mannishly tailored at collar and cuffs, most becoming over her pale, fine-boned form. Her silvery hair was longer than I remembered it, and she had it tied back loosely at the nape of her neck, secured with a long brown and orange paisley scarf. Thinking of the cart track outside Rook's Cottage I glanced at her feet: russet suede boots. The trouble was my wife simply did not know how *not* to be elegant. Her hands, long and pale and utterly still, lay in her lap.

When she spoke her voice surprised me. I had been studying her as you would a painting, and was as startled as if some exquisite portrait had suddenly found a voice.

'Tyrrell sends his love.'

'I feel guilty, I haven't written.'

'Well you haven't been down here long.' She was right, of course, but to me it seemed a lifetime. I realised that I had been in another world, experiencing time in a different way, but I could not explain this to Elise.

'He hopes that I'll take you back with me,' she went on, not looking at me, staring out of the side window at the hills with their chequered bedspread of fields.

'I'm afraid I shan't come up to expectation in that case,' I said as gently as possible, but there was no reaction.

She gave a little shrug. '*Tant pis.*' I wondered if she really couldn't have cared less or whether this was one of her carefully simulated poses.

We hardly spoke for the rest of the journey, though the air was humming with things that needed to be said. As we drove down through Ballacombe, I remarked: 'This is it.'

'It's just as I imagined.'

'Really? I thought you might be disappointed.'

'Oh no, darling, I didn't pitch my hopes too high.' I realised she was laughing at me, and smiled back.

'It's not exactly golden thatch and climbing roses, is it?'

'No, but it has a character of its own.' We began to climb the hill out of the village on the other side.

'Wait till you see the cottage,' I said.

'It's not pretty?'

I shook my head. 'No. It's plain and prim and square.'

'An old maid house.'

Typical Elise.

'If you like.'

Within minutes we had reached the turning to Rook's Cottage. I glanced at my wife but her face gave away nothing as the wheels of the Morris churned and spun in the rutted mud. The air in the makeshift garage felt clammy and smelt of damp as we got out.

'Shall we leave the cases for a moment till we've had a drink and some lunch?' I ventured.

'Perhaps I could just have the small one.'

'Of course.' As I hauled open the creaking boot I thought how typical of Elise it was to want that one, small case – an aptly named 'vanity' case. Even here in the moist, silent everydayness of Ballacombe she could not relax until she had glanced into a mirror, patted her sleek hair and made a few token 'moues' with that exquisite glossy mouth. I took the case and preceded her out of the garage, over the wet path and in at the back door of Rook's Cottage.

To my relief, the kitchen was warm, and the aroma of the extremely plain stew I had put in the oven before leaving was persuasive and appetising – at least to me, now used to my own plain fare.

'This is the kitchen,' I remarked unnecessarily, and Elise gazed round, smiling to herself, saying nothing. 'Come upstairs and I'll show you your room.'

'Your room too?' she asked, as she followed me up the stairs.

'I'm afraid not, there are just the three bedrooms and they're very small, certainly not room for two beds.'

'As long as it's nothing personal.'

Since when, I pondered ruefully, has it mattered very much to you? I opened the door of her room, identical to mine in its monastic austerity, but overlooking the garden and the fields beyond.

'Is it alright?'

'Of course.' She turned with her most beautiful smile and held out her arms. I was charmed, entranced and went to her willingly. She felt slender, warm, sweetly yielding. She smelt like a flower. I wished that her hair was loose so that I could nuzzle into it, feel it sliding between my fingers, but the habit of restraint was too entrenched and I contented myself with stroking it.

'Let's stay up here for a while,' I whispered, and felt her shake her head gently against my neck. 'Why not?'

'Because and because and because.'

'Not good enough. I want you, I've missed you—'

'No.' She stepped back, her fingers resting lightly on my shoulders. 'You most certainly have not.'

'Why do you say that?' I felt, and sounded, aggrieved, but I was aware that my question was not entirely without hypocrisy. I had not missed Elise, I was simply aware of what I had done without now that she was standing here in front of me. But far from tugging at my heart strings inspiring me with thoughts of home, she was like a creature from some strange and distant civilisation.

Now she shrugged a little Gallic shrug, one of the very few native mannerisms she sparingly permitted herself. 'If you don't know then there is no point in telling. Shall we have something to eat?' We went downstairs, our footsteps together but not in time.

After lunch we walked a little way and then returned and sat out in the garden of Rook's Cottage still on our coats in the cold afternoon sunshine in some old folding canvas beach chairs I had discovered in the garden shed. Until then our conversation had remained resolutely trivial – Elise had expressed nicely modulated pleasure at the prospect of going to the Dellers, and I had told her about the local mystery concerning Holz, and the missing girl. This story unexpectedly charmed her.

'How extraordinary! And is the man guilty?'

'I've no idea. I choose to think not.'

'Ah! Already you're taking sides.'

'No, there are no sides to take, the whole case is way back in the past.'

'But soon to be resurrected, as you point out, by the demon journalist.'

'Well –' I said what I was very far from feeling, 'I don't think he'll do any lasting harm, he's only a small-time hack.'

'You don't like him one bit.'

'No. But that has nothing to do with it.'

'Of course not.'

'Anyway, it's only a small local thing, nothing earth-shaking – but it's surprising how quickly things like that absorb you in a village where there's not much else to think about.'

'I'm sure I should be fascinated.'

I debated whether to tell her of my own experiences with regard to the affair, but rejected the idea almost instantly. Indeed I was beginning to hug my visions to myself with a miserly protectiveness, hoarding them jealously against some hypothetical occasion when they would make every-thing clear. To change the subject I enquired about college, about Tyrrell and my students.

'Bob's well. He still thinks you're crazy.'

'*What?*' I did not realise how striking my overreac-tion had been till I saw Elise's brows arch in surprise. The word 'crazy' had struck me like a blow, yet it had been intended as no more than a casual, lighthearted comment.

'He thinks you're doing the wrong thing.'

'It's none of his business.'

'It's his cottage.'

'Which he offered to me. So what does he intend to

do? Turn me out and pack me back to town like a naughty boy?'

'You know he wouldn't. It's just that he feels –' here she spread her slim fingers on her knees and bent to study them as though looking for gold – 'that we should be here together.'

'And here we are.'

'From the start.'

'I refuse to go through all that again.'

'As far as I am concerned –' she did not look up but her voice was hard – 'you have never been through it once.'

'Nonsense, Elise, I explained—'

'You explained to no one!' Now she raised her eyes and they were cold and bitter. Ironically it was the most passionate I was ever to see her. 'You treat me like a fool, like a child, I look foolish to all our friends. I cannot understand why you should behave like this.'

'You couldn't help,' I said lamely.

'How do you know? You haven't told me anything.'

'I can't.'

'Why?'

'Because and because and because!' I spat her words back at her in a sudden fit of miserable rage. They hung in the stillness of the garden. To my amazement it was Elise who made the first step toward conciliation.

'Let's go back together – nothing to do with Bob – let's decide we can make things better together, it only needs a decision.' Her voice was as soft and cool as her skin, drops of water on the fire of my rage. But when I looked at her, sitting there like some exotic flower transplanted from Kew to this drab country plot I realised that I could not – perhaps would not – ever go back with her.

Somehow over the past two weeks I had simply become part of what was here. My increasingly strong sense of involvement and responsibility in the local melodrama wrapped me about like a shroud; and like a corpse I stared at my wife and said nothing. It seemed to me that she had only come – that I had only asked her – in order to say good-bye. I had never intended to heal the rift, never intended to return, or make amends or to pick up the threads of my old life in any way. I was saying good-bye to Elise, watching her with more and more detachment as the slow, country minutes ticked away; the delicate web of civilised urban marriage was tearing silently, dissolving to shreds and blowing away and we were left, two separate, sorrowful beings stripped of our comforting conventions.

I shook my head. Elise went into the cottage without a word.

Such is force of habit that somehow we got through the evening, even conversing a little, and I was for the ump-teenth time astonished by my wife's resilience. For one of the few occasions in her life she had dropped her guard, set herself at my mercy, and been rebuffed. And yet she had picked herself up, dusted herself off and was now able to cook soufflé omelette in these unfamiliar surroundings with all the aplomb in the world. Her panache could almost have won me over. But when we went up to bed, early at ten o'clock, I kissed her cheek and let her go to her room across the narrow landing with no sensation but relief.

After only twenty minutes I heard the click and saw the sudden dark of her lamp going off. But I had not even undressed. Instead I stood by the window and gazed out at the darkening view which had become familiar. It was like looking at a picture inside my head, so intimately did I now know it. Quite naturally – it hardly needed a conscious decision – I left my room, slipped down the stairs and went out of the front door.

The darkness did not seem so intense now that I was out

in it, part of it. And as always I turned right, away from the road and down the lane, but I hadn't gone a few paces before I became conscious of someone coming up behind me. I say 'became conscious' for it was really no more precise than that. I did not hear steps, nor see anything until the person had drawn level with me, and though he carried before him the bright disc of a torch, it shed no heralding beam in front of it. Besides this the man did not appear to notice me at all, I might have been a ghost standing there in the middle of the narrow lane. It was Holz.

The now-familiar profile stood out clear against the night for two full seconds as he passed me, and then the dark seemed to swallow the solid blackness of his back view. For some reason I found myself short of breath and slightly sick. The shock, I told myself, of nearly colliding with someone in the dark, but even so I felt dread, and the far-off whine in the distance of my inner brain that meant I was falling . . . falling . . .

Desperate, panicking, I stumbled forward in the darkness which now seemed as heavy as a cloth cast over my head, holding out my hands before me like a blind man, determined to catch up with Holz, to grasp the cloth of his jacket, stare into his eyes, ascertain that he was flesh and blood. But though I sometimes seemed to see a mass of greater black in the darkness I encountered no one. A sudden lightening to my left reminded me that I was now parallel with the gateway to the ploughed field and I instinctively turned towards it and crashed into the rough crossbars, gripping the top one, my eyes straining to see – my ears to hear.

And then there was something else. The singing in my ears was as sharp and painful as a laser. I clapped my palms to the sides of my head to stifle it, turning and stumbling in the darkness like a foolish blindfold dancing bear trying to locate his tormentors. Yes, there was something else –

again no sound, no sight, but there was a movement in the air – a swirl and eddy like the surface of a pool when an otter dives, a coolness against my face as it rushed, as someone ran by me along the side of the field, so close he almost brushed my face with his shoulder. I saw, or had an impression of, a chalk-white face, a tall, slim figure – a young man – and the pounding of a heart dilated with terror, filling the night with its shuddering pulse. And yet not a sound. I can best describe it as a movement, a sensation, so strong, so fearful that it was engraved on the air. And just before the blackness of the night became the blackness of unconsciousness I saw Holz again, a black pillar in the centre of the plough, still and threatening.

I had seen the victim. That was my first thought as I came to, clammy with fear and nausea, my face bruised where I had fallen against the lichened bars of the gate. I had seen again the killer and his prey, only this time closer, the time was nearer, and now I knew who it was that I had to warn. For I was certain I had seen Austen.

Dragging myself to my feet, fighting off the terrible dizziness, it seemed to me that the night was lighter, and that though secretive and silent as a tomb only minutes ago, it was once more alive with the nocturnal noises of the country, an almost deafening cacophony of life and business, small feet stirring the first dead leaves at the side of the lane, wings fluttering in the dense hedge, twigs crackling, a nightjar chittering, the bark of a vixen up on the hill by the church path. Sick and confused, I stumbled back towards the cottage.

'Are you alright, Mr Bowater?' I heard the voice just as the long cylindrical beam of the torch swam into my range of vision, and the dry patter and click of a dog's paws came up to me.

I looked up, shielding my eyes against the light which was now deferentially turned aside.

It was Holz.

He stood there in front of me, totally unaware of the effect he was having. His face displayed nothing but polite concern. He wore a white fisherman's sweater and carried a length of rope, while round my legs pattered a black and tan mongrel, amiable and curious. 'I was walking my dog,' said Holz. 'But you don't look at all well.'

'Oh, I'm alright.' My voice boomed in my ears, grotesque and artificial. 'As a matter of fact I did feel a little faint – I came out to get some air. I'm better now.'

'Good, good. Well I'll be on my way. Oh, and by the way –'

'Yes?' I realised that I was terrified of him, expecting a blow, a shock.

'Mr Tyrrell pays me to keep an eye on the garden at Rook's Cottage – there's very little planted this year but I keep it tidy – may I come this week?'

'Come when you like.'

'Would it be alright if I let myself in and do the work next time I have the chance?'

'Yes, yes.' I was starting to walk away and I could see the look of curiosity on his face before the darkness came between us and he said: 'Good-night, Mr Bowater.'

Ten

On Friday evening we prepared to go to the Dellers. It was a bizarre charade, me shaving on the landing, my electric shaver suspended from the light socket, Elise sitting at the tiny window table in her room putting on her make-up with meticulous care. What were we doing? I asked myself. This wasn't real, it had nothing to do with *us*, the people we were, the feelings and thoughts we so assiduously concealed. I had told Elise nothing of my walk the previous night, but this morning she had been up early, and when I had finally staggered to the kitchen there was something in her manner, composed, yet watchful, which prepared me for the question which inevitably came over the second cup of coffee.

'Whatever were you doing last night?'

'I'm sorry, did I wake you?'

'Yes, but you know I'm a light sleeper. You were ill.'

'No –'

'I heard you, you were sick.' I was appalled at the thought of Elise listening to my prolonged retching.

'I'm sorry.'

'There's no need. But I was worried about you. I only didn't come out because I knew you'd rather cope alone.'

'That's true. As a matter of fact I was feeling a little queasy earlier on, that's why I went out, but unfortunately—'

'It did no good.' She was staring at me steadily over the rim of her cup. 'I hope it was nothing you ate.'

'Of course not.' I tried a reassuring smile.

'I think,' said Elise, turning her head to look out of the window as though she were about to comment on the weather, 'that something happened.'

'Happened?'

'While you were out. One of your turns – you saw something, felt something. The way you do.' There was the faintest note of irony in her voice which dispelled any lurking inclination I might have had to tell her what had occurred. It was odd the way she continually came within an ace of winning me over yet always, ultimately, failed. Or drew back. We were jinxed, I thought, and then added mentally that that was typical of my melodramatic frame of mind at the moment.

And so the subject had been closed and the day had passed – quite a pleasant day out in the country, driving about, a couple of unchallenging walks, lunch in a pub, a day during which we might have been a couple of amicable acquaintances rather than man and wife. We were polite, cautious, anxious to please each other not because we cared that much but because we wanted tranquillity, and a quiet life.

My desire for Elise had wilted and withered since its brief flowering the previous day. Now she held about as much attraction for me as a plaster Victorian doll – beautiful, delicate, marvellously bedecked and painted, but basically lifeless.

She had put on a narrow, apple-green shift of wild silk, as simple and stunning as an ear of young corn, above which the clean lines of her patrician neck and sleek head rose like those on a coin. Her skin was always pale – she regarded brown skin as both vulgar and unhealthy – but it had been nourished and cared for for so many years that it never had that unwholesome look that so many white skins have. It was smoothly luminous and cool. When my hand lay for a moment on her bare arm as we got into the car it looked unspeakable, like the paw of some great rough animal on the skin of a child, so that I withdrew it quickly, experiencing a shock as though I had seen myself changing from Jekyll to Hyde.

I knew at once that Elise was Diana the huntress that evening. As we drove up the hill to Deller House there was a sparkle about her, a crackle of mischievous excitement which I recognised. At home in London I should have been filled with foreboding by these manifestations which usually heralded a sophisticated display of social games-manship, but here I was simply relieved that she was going to occupy herself, that she was interested enough to play her games, leaving me to observe and reflect and withdraw into myself as I had done more and more recently. And, I had to admit, I wanted the chance to talk to Susan. Once I had been the outsider, regarding Susan with the curiosity of all other outsiders. Now, I was on her side, with her against the rest though she herself might not know it.

To my intense relief Austen was not present when we arrived at the house, and was obviously not expected. I did not know how I would have looked him in the eye. I supposed that I should have to tell him of my presentiment and yet the thought of facing that neat, feline face and announcing what I believed to be its fate appalled me.

The weight of this morbid, self-imposed responsibility hung on me like a millstone. I was a dead weight in the cheerful, social atmosphere, the bright small talk washing round me like so many inconsequential ripples round a rock.

Elise was a success. Within minutes Arnold was putting his arm round her waist and flirting with her in his agree-able, obvious way, and Marjorie was all smiles, captivated by my wife's charm. But most strange of all, Susan also worshipped at the shrine. And if anything she worshipped with greater fervour than her parents. My hopes of talking to her alone while Elise held the floor with Arnold and Marjorie were bitterly dashed. Susan appeared to have eyes for no one but Elise. Her face mirrored Elise's smiles and frowns, her eyes followed her everywhere, there was a lightness – even frivolity – in her manner which I could not recall ever having noticed before. I thought (rather churlishly, since it was the factor which isolated her from me) that it became her ill. She appeared to my jaundiced eyes slightly silly, like a large grim-faced woman at Blackpool wearing one of those ludicrous seaside hats. It was not her style, not the Susan I knew at all. And yet it did remind me of something, it echoed a previous impression from somewhere which I could not place.

Elise in her turn made herself pleasing to Susan. I had never known her behave badly, to be rude, or indifferent or ignore a person – the niceties of etiquette were bred into the very marrow of her bones, but by this time I thought I knew when she was being sincere and when simply going through the motions. And to my astonishment it appeared that this performance was for real. At least, I could detect an element of tenderness in it, an almost maternal gentleness which I should not have expected her to feel for Susan. She had a fastidious dislike of women who did not make the best of themselves, no matter what their natural advantages. She gave no quarter in the matter of sloppy dress, ill-kempt hair and the like – it amazed me the vituperative energy she could put into the criticism of such trivia when disasters on a grander scale barely ruffled her calm.

Yet here she was, seated on the sofa beside Susan, listening to her earnestly, nodding and smiling as though encouraging a shy but endearing child while Marjorie sat on the sidelines occasionally putting her oar in, otherwise content to gaze fondly.

Arnold Deller, however, did not attempt to disguise his surprise at this unlooked-for alliance. His gratification was rather touching, even pathetic. This great bluff, tough man had spent half a lifetime pussyfooting warily round his daughter. Her oddness had at once endeared her to, and estranged her from, him. He had had to learn the meaning of loneliness, the agonising blunders of shyness and eccentricity, as foreign to his nature as the tribal customs of some primitive people.

'Your wife's grand,' he said to me confidentially, indicating with a sideways nod Elise and Susan. 'Really grand, I mean that. I haven't seen our Sue so relaxed in years. How does she do it?'

'It's an art,' I said, and meant it.

'It's that alright. And she's a lovely woman, too,' he added, as though recommending her for a sale. 'You don't see many like that these days, it's all the natural look and in most cases nature could do with improving on.' I had to smile. 'I like a woman who knows how to present herself. Marjorie's always done that and it's what I like to see – a bit of style, a bit of class, not all this take-me-as-you-find-me-and-make-the-best-of-it attitude.'

'She is French – it's bred into her.'

'But the charm, the charm . . .' He shook his head in disbelief. 'Sue's not easy, you know, not easy at all.' He looked at me anxiously, as though expecting me to launch a vindictive attack.

'I think she's lovely,' I said truthfully, and he must have caught the sincerity in my voice for he beamed, after a brief moment of suspicion.

'She's a good girl. I'll be truthful, sometimes I've no idea what goes on in her mind, she's as secret as a grave, not like a girl of her age at all. When I think of Marge – she was that age when I first met her, but just the opposite, real one for the boys she was, always laughing and having fun. And when I look at the young girls today – most of them look more sophisticated at fourteen than Susan does now.'

'That's not necessarily a virtue. I find it rather dismaying.'

'It's a comfort to hear you say so, but you understand what I mean – a father wants to see his daughter have fun, enjoying things while she's young, looking pretty, going out with boys.'

'You'd probably worry to death that she was being promiscuous.' I understood his anxiety precisely but it was obvious that he sought reassurance rather than advice or analysis, and the matter of Susan was a sensitive subject with me as well. I wished to fend off his paternal confidences before he told me something that shook me.

'If you want my opinion,' I said, adopting a jocular man-to-man tone, 'I think her originality makes her very attractive. Count yourself lucky.'

'You're probably right.' He still looked slightly anxious, so I passed him my glass.

'I'd like another if I may.'

'Of course, do forgive me. I was getting bogged down in my old codger stuff.'

On his return I was ready with a change of subject. 'How's Mr Austen getting on with his investigation?' I asked.

'I don't know.' My host looked serious. 'And I'm not sure I want to know. The whole thing worries me. I don't go for all this digging up old dirt. Isn't there a quotation "old, unhappy far-off things"? That's the way I feel about it. The whole business is in the past, let's leave it there. Besides, I shall lose a good gardener.'

The quiet, matter-of-fact tone of his voice caught me

off guard for a moment, so that I didn't absorb the precise matter of what he had said. When I did, it gave me a cold shock.

'Why do you say that?'

'Young Ambrose thinks it was him.'

It was so exactly what I had expected to hear him say that I could think of nothing by way of reply. After a brief silence Deller went on: 'He says he can't point the finger direct, there's no new evidence, he's just been persuaded by local opinion and so on. Local gossip I'd call it. I'm disappointed in the boy. He's bright but he's still too impressionable.'

This was not an opinion I could let pass unchallenged.

'On the contrary, I think he's calculating.'

'How so?'

'I think he's a good pressman – unemotional, objective, he knows when he's got a good story.'

'But it won't stand up.'

'Not legally, but you said yourself, he's not trying to make a legal case. It'll be trial and sentence by innuendo. "Ex-Nazi Loner Condemned Out of Villagers' Own Mouths", that sort of thing. It'll be as damaging as anything that happens in a court of law – more so, because it'll be indefensible.'

'And he'll do it on purpose – do you think he really believes Holz is guilty?'

'That's immaterial. Guilt is good copy. But he ought to be damn careful, he's playing with fire.'

'He'll get away with it, the press always do,' said Deller gloomily.

'He may not be punished officially, but there's always the personal factor.'

'You mean revenge?' His tone was incredulous, and this infuriated me. They were all so slow, so complacent, they never expected anyone to get hurt.

Even so, my voice sounded harder than intended as I said, 'Just that.'

'Beating him up.'

'Or murder.' The word was out before I could stop it, it dropped into the silence between us like the hideous evidence of a crime – a knife, a bloodstain. It seemed extraordinary that the group on the sofa, Elise, Susan and Marjorie, could continue chatting as though nothing had happened. The air hummed with what I had just said.

It must have been two minutes before Deller replied: 'Are you actually saying that Ambrose might be killed because of what he would say in the paper?'

'It's not impossible.'

'It preys on your mind.'

'It does. I was in the pub with Austen the other morning when Holz spoke to us.'

'He threatened?'

'No.'

'I didn't think so, he's the quietest, most—'

'Quietness means nothing. The most appallingly violent crimes have been committed by quiet, soft-spoken men. No, he didn't threaten. He was dignified and he warned.'

'That sounds more like it. Even so it's not like him to intervene. He keeps himself to himself, maintains a low profile. It's one of the reasons these people don't trust him.'

We both fell silent, each preoccupied with his own point of view. Whole realms of threat of strangeness and danger had opened before us. Nothing was what it had seemed. And the three women still sitting there in their bright dresses, two blonde heads and one dark, were like flowers nodding in the bleak wind of an otherwise strange and fearful landscape. Outside, the twilight was smoky and autumnal. I went to the window and stood gazing at the huge, formal garden as its bright daylight tones were washed to grey

by the creeping evening, and its neat, civilised outlines
smudged.

Suddenly Elise was at my side, her soft voice was
very close.

'I think it's time we went.'

'Very well.'

She turned away again to face Marjorie, who was
approaching, and said: 'My dear, I think we should be
going.'

'But you only just got here! I was about to ask you to
stay and have something to eat.'

'How sweet of you, but actually I did leave something
in the oven.' I didn't know whether this was true or not.
'I think we'll get back, but perhaps we'll see you again,
it's been so pleasant.'

'It has indeed.' Arnold joined us and I was conscious of
Susan standing on the fringe of the group, her arms clasped
across her middle. She always gave the impression that she
needed pockets into which to thrust those large hands, and
boots in which to stride out over springy grass. I had not
spoken a word to her all evening. As my wife and the
Dellers exchanged niceties I tried to catch her eyes but
she was staring at Elise. Probably imagining that no one
was watching her, that stare was as naked as the day
– a stare of hunger, of longing, at once powerful yet
naïve. The primitively acquisitive stare of a child who
gazes into a shop window. I looked away again hurriedly,
embarrassed to have seen. I could only assume that the
heady brew of my wife's beauty and charm had roused in
Susan an admiration and envy that she had never before
been moved to feel. This, I thought, was something that
Susan considered worth aiming for. Not the second-rate
sophistication of trendy teenagers and brittle career girls,
but the genuine article, as glossy and impressive as a Rolls
Royce. I wished that I could have told her how sad the

reality was, and how little worth aspiring to was the whole chilly, fragile façade.

We left. In the car, Elise remarked: 'Let's go somewhere to eat.'

'There's nothing in the oven then?'

She didn't answer the question, but said, rather bleakly, 'It was time to go.'

'We'd been there less than an hour.'

'Quite long enough for a casual drink.'

'Certainly. But they're very hospitable people –'

'I know. I realise that. They were delightful, kindness itself, the salt of the earth.'

'They genuinely admire you.'

'Yes.' She turned on me those pale grey eyes, clear as water. 'Especially Susan.'

'She's a strange girl. I like her.'

'I know. In fact she's quite ensnared you, hasn't she, with her healthy outdoor charm and her buxom figure.' Elise's voice was acid. She surely was not jealous? Elise jealous? But no it wasn't that, there was irony in her manner, some peculiar wry amusement at the bitterness of life.

'Elise, why are you being like this? What are they to you?'

'They're nothing to me, my darling Michael. But you have such a soft spot for the quaint Susan, and she –' she looked at me appraisingly – 'far prefers women.'

Of course. Why is that so often one's reaction to the most shattering revelations? They are shattering simply because they have been there all the time, only barely under the surface of life, just discernible but unidentified, things that we may even have guessed at in the dark caves of our minds but pushed back again before we saw properly, not choosing to know.

Of course Susan 'preferred women' as Elise chose to put

it. I was not horrified, just overcome by a great sadness – for Susan, for myself, for Elise, for the Dellers – even, for some strange reason, for Holz, who was such a friend to Susan because he himself understood loneliness. And I thought, with a touch of maudlin self-pity for my attempts to get close to her and ingratiate myself, of my little sensations of pride when I won her confidence for a few minutes, or felt myself to be in sympathy. The sort of pride one gets from being greeted by a half-wild animal or a capricious child. The winding road swam in front of me so that I was obliged to pull over and stop the engine. And there we sat in the gathering dusk as foolish and nonplussed as two deserted children. I became aware that Elise was still speaking, her voice was trickling away next to me, soft but persistent.

'Poor Michael, such a romantic and you have to pick a girl who would rather have your wife.' She was not being cruel – her tone was tender rather than mocking but even its tenderness discomforted me. 'She's not without appeal, either.'

'What do you mean?' I suddenly thought with horror of the possibility of Susan and Elise, and Elise must have read my thoughts for she smiled a wry smile.

'Oh, don't worry. Whatever my shortcomings as a wife I don't as yet look to my own sex for reassurance.' I had never before heard her admit any weakness and it really unmanned me.

'Elise—'

'It's alright.' She pushed my hand away with a little pat. 'And anyway one shouldn't assume that someone is promiscuous simply because they're homosexual.'

'You sound like a medical manual.'

'I'm sorry, but it's true. The girl was merely reacting to me in the way *you* might stand admiringly by the side of some gorgeous young thing at a party. Perfectly harmless and innocent, it's just that the message is plain for any woman to read.'

'It explains a lot.'

'I'm sure.'

Because it was sad sitting there, and because there seemed nothing else to say, I started up the car and we began once more to follow the curve of the road down to Ballacombe.

'Where shall we go?' I asked.

'Anywhere. I'm not hungry, I just don't want to go back yet.'

'We'll find a pub.'

'Pubs. We went to a pub at lunch time too. I feel rootless.'

'Well –'

'No, no, it's a good idea. I don't want to go back to that cottage.'

I drove into Ballacombe and then turned right, out along a road I did not know. The village looked bleak and closed, just as it had done on that first evening when I had come through it in the torrential summer rain. I felt that I knew now why so many people feared and mistrusted the country, why they preferred the hubbub and stress of cities to the 'peace and quiet' offered by places like Ballacombe. They preferred it because the country was secretive and dour and hugged its thoughts to itself. The bland fields lay like a dust sheet over furniture, disguising and concealing, and the faces of the cottages were closed – they watched but could not be watched.

Elise pointed out of her window. 'An estate. How funny.'

I slowed down and glanced out at the neat grid of modern council homes on the hillside. 'Why funny?' I asked, though I knew what she meant.

'It's so un-rural, somehow.'

'Not every country person can live in a thatched paradise.'

'No but . . . I don't know.' We drove on. But I remembered as we left the estate behind us on the left, and Ballacombe trickling down into its valley on the right, that Cyril Thorne had told me Jan Holz had a council house. Perhaps – and it was evidence of my compulsive involvement – I could have a word with Holz?

I don't know what I intended to do or say. But now that I knew where Holz lived I felt almost as though I had been directed to his door. I must go, I must try. Perhaps just by talking the sore could be cauterised.

'Did you plan anything special tomorrow?' I asked casually.

'No. But Marjorie Deller invited me to have some lunch and see their garden if I wanted to. Would you like me to do that?'

'Yes – no!' She had trapped me into saying I wanted her out of the way. I glanced at her but she was looking out of the window and her voice was level.

'I think I shall go, it's a beautiful garden. You do as you wish.'

I did not attempt to exonerate myself, my efforts would simply have been clumsy and more hurtful. I left it at that, and determined to find Holz the next day.

Eleven

I did not drive the car right up to the estate the next day but parked it at the bottom of the hill and walked. I did not want to be conspicuous and shamefacedly admitted to myself that some of Holz's unpopularity might rub off on me if I were seen visiting his home. However, I soon enough realised that I should have to give myself away since I hadn't the faintest idea which was Holz's house. The estate was not large and the Avenues, Ways and Drives were laid out in a tidy grid pattern on the surface of the fields. It was peaceful, children played on the pavements and a last-chance ice-cream van tinkled tunefully in the near distance. A woman was out in her garden hanging washing on a line.

'Excuse me –'

She looked up, bright, neighbourly, enquiring.

'Have you any idea where a Mr Jan Holz lives?' She answered right away without comment or hesitation, but her expression changed. Her eyes became watchful and suspicious and as I walked away in the direction she had indicated, I was conscious of her following me with those eyes, wondering about me, remembering to mention me when next she got together with a friend.

When I came to Holz's house I knew I couldn't have missed it. The garden stood out like a diamond in a pile of pebbles, bright with flowers, not formal and smart, but a cheerful profusion of living things, a mass of colour and vitality. The spectacle of such natural abundance contrasted oddly with my picture of Holz – so reserved and stern and ascetic, so intensely dignified. Then I remembered the beautiful little carved otter that Susan Deller had shown me, the wood warm and glossy like the animal it depicted, and I knew that the real Jan Holz had long been buried deep beneath a defence as impregnable as steel. I opened the gate and as I walked up the path an ugly, friendly dog came round the side of the house to greet me, the same dog which had pattered round my legs in the dark the other night . . .

As I reached the door it opened before me and I saw Holz's tall figure in the twilight of the narrow hall.

'Will you come in, Mr Bowater?' He drew back the door and I stepped in, uncomfortable because he had seen me coming, anticipated my movements and so taken the initiative.

'What can I do for you?' he asked as we both stood there with the eager mongrel's affable panting filling the small space between us.

'I wondered . . . if I could have a chat with you.'

'Of course. Anything in particular?' I couldn't see the look in his eyes and his voice gave away nothing. I began to flounder.

'It's a little hard to explain. I'm afraid you'll think me mad . . .' The word faded on my lips but hung like a ghost in the air. After all, what had I come to say? To accuse him of murder? For that was what it amounted to. I am mad, I thought, or I would never be here.

'Come in,' said Holz, opening the door to the left of the hallway.

'Perhaps I'd better go.'

'But why?'

'I'm afraid I shan't be able to make myself understood without giving you offence or appearing crazy.'

'You underestimate me, Mr Bowater. I am long past being easily offended and as to the other, I thought the English said that people in glass houses shouldn't throw stones?'

'I don't see—'

He laughed, a short dry laugh, the first and the last I was ever to hear from him. 'I mean that I am near enough mad myself to know that one person's madness is another's sanity. Come in.'

I took it as an order and went into the little sitting room. It was bright and pleasant, with a window that overlooked the small back garden. The latter, as far as I could make out, was entirely given over to fruit and vegetables and a giant green wall of runner beans afforded complete privacy from the garden which backed on to it. I was reminded of the tangled green forest which had wrapped around the castle of the sleeping beauty, and a picture I had had of the inside of that castle with the characters arrested in their actions, fast asleep beneath a shroud of cobwebs, the embracing greenery poking leaves through every chink in the walls and windows . . .

'You see beans are not only good to eat.' He interrupted my thoughts pleasantly enough and I turned back to him. In this lighter room I had a chance to look properly at his sad, long face, 'a violin face' Elise would have called it, and his fine hands, the fingers spread like tentacles over the back of the chair he leaned on. Hands for making things, for conjuring up greenness and lushness, for carving and stroking. And for making love, I would have added but that I knew this man had no one to love but his dog and a lonely girl who could not love him.

'Would you like some tea?'

'Do you—?'

'I usually have some in the afternoon.'

'Thank you.'

He left quietly and I had the opportunity to look around. The foolishly friendly dog came and pressed against my legs, his rough chin resting on my knee.

There were carvings everywhere. It was as though Holz the artist had tried to create from wood the world in which he was denied a part. And the carvings were not only of animals. Animals there were, and birds, even the ugly bandy-legged pooch was depicted with charm and humour. But there were also people, most of them busy about some chore or other, fat women carrying washing, children absorbed in a game on the ground, men chopping and running and throwing. The overall effect of so many statuettes in a small space might have been claustrophobic, and that it was not was due to the fact that the rest of the room was starkly plain, a typical solitary person's room. Clean, neat, and empty but for two hard chairs (on one of which I was seated), a large trestle table and a hideous old sideboard loaded with books, oddments and a large old-fashioned radio. There were no pictures, no photographs and, oddly, no flowers.

As Holz re-entered I said: 'You must love flowers. Your garden's magnificent.'

'Thank you. You're wondering why I have none in this room. I don't like to see wild things tamed and captured, serving out a life sentence so that we can display our proficiency at killing.'

'But surely a few flowers – what else are they for?'

'They are for beauty, I agree. But I prefer to see them out of doors.' I glanced out at his brilliant front garden and was obliged to admit that he was right. The flowers there seemed to possess life, nodding and rustling and leaning together like a bright company of beautifully dressed people at a wedding.

Holz handed me a white enamel mug full of strong tea and sat down on the other hard chair. He sat very erect, his back against the back, his feet planted firmly on the ground. 'So,' he said. It was an invitation for me to begin. I looked into his face and found it solemn, intent, but not unfriendly. I realised that there would be little point in being evasive. I took a long mouthful of the scalding tea and then launched on my extraordinary statement.

'You won't know – though you may have guessed – that I came down here because I was unwell.'

'I had not guessed.'

'Thank you, but I feel sure that my state of mind is apparent. In London I had something like a nervous breakdown, I was shattered and frightened. I simply felt that I wanted to escape from all that I knew and from all who knew me, that even included my wife. At any rate I won't go into all that too much. The point is that instead of an immediate improvement I almost at once experienced another hallucination of the kind which had upset me in London.'

'Hallucination?'

'Hallucination, premonition – I believe that in London I saw evidence of something before it actually happened.'

If I had expected Holz to react in any way I was mistaken. He displayed no interest beyond that which would normally be afforded a talkative visitor out of politeness. He did not speak, but his eyes remained on me, quiet and level and secret. I had to blunder on with no idea of the effect I was having on my audience.

'I thought I saw – I did see – evidence of the suicide of one of my best students, several days before the tragedy occurred.'

Still no flicker of vulgar curiosity. My vanity was piqued.

'I have to know whether you believe me. Otherwise there is no point in my going on.'

'I believe that you saw what you saw.' His voice was even.

'Well then . . .' I was unconvinced. 'I was terrified, panic-stricken, my nerves went to pieces and I came down here to recuperate and take stock. However, as I said, I have since experienced another of these extraordinary visions.'

'And this time?'

I had long since decided that it was pointless to put off the moment of truth when it arrived. 'I believe that I saw you kill someone.'

I did not look at him for a second or two, and when I did I saw that he appeared baffled rather than horrified.

'Tell me about it.' I had to give him full marks for cool. It was as though he had absorbed so many shocks in his life that he had developed an immunity.

'You don't think me a hysteric?'

'I don't hold opinions of that kind. I take things at their face value. You tell me you have foreseen me killing someone. I immediately find myself wondering who it is I might want to kill.' Something must have showed on my face for he added, 'I shock you.'

'You're very direct.'

He smiled. 'But I can think of no one about whom I care enough.'

'No one?'

'Mr Bowater –' Holz leaned forward – 'am I to understand that you come here with a theory?'

'Not a theory, no. But I must be honest. Last time I felt sure I had "seen" the victim as well, and on reflection it seemed – well so appallingly logical. It was Ambrose Austen.'

'Ah.' It was no more than a little sigh in the silence. The angular face remained undisturbed by any display of emotion. When he spoke, it was still quite evenly. 'So – you think you saw me kill the journalist.'

'That's right.'

'Stab him with a knife – in a field by the church path, right?'

I nodded. But mockingly he shook his head and the faintest smile curved his mouth but didn't reach his eyes.

'No, Mr Bowater. I'm sorry to have to tell you that your dream won't come true. I have no intention of doing anything so dramatic as to murder Mr Austen.'

'I wasn't suggesting that you might actually be planning it at this moment. I accuse you of nothing—'

'I'm glad of that.'

'I merely felt that I had to tell you – for you to be on your guard, to do nothing rash.' In exasperation I rose, and almost shouted. 'For God's sake, man, try to believe me. It's so real to me, so *real!*'

'I do believe you.' He also stood and the dog whined softly, looking from one to the other anxiously. 'I believe you saw what you saw. But in turn you must believe that Austen means nothing to me. A poet of yours said, "For each man kills the thing he loves." We do not kill where we do not care. I doubt, though I cannot be certain, that I am a murderer by nature, but if I were I haven't yet found my victim. And I don't believe in predestination.'

'I see.'

'I can see you're disappointed.'

'Well – hardly. I'd be a lunatic if I wanted you to go out and kill someone simply to prove me right. It's just that I feel so sure . . .' I tailed off, unable to take my frail case any further. I felt suddenly tired, weak and depressed. 'I must go.'

Holz showed me to the door, and this time the dog did not follow him but remained in the living room, where it lay down and rested its arrow-shaped muzzle on its forepaws in a contemplative pose. Its round, bright black pebble eyes were fixed on us, its whole body was tense as though it were about to spring. I was fearful and agitated.

All I wanted to do was to leave this house, this strange man and his watchful dog.

When we reached the door Holz began to say something and I thought I felt his light touch on my sleeve, but a sickening panic grabbed me by the throat and I burst from the door like a drowning man into the sunlight, and staggered down the path, not looking behind me.

As I blundered back to the car the blind panic ebbed but the fear remained, and with it a bleak misery that I hadn't known since I was a child: the misery of frustration and loneliness. There was nobody who understood. All my sense of what was right, the comforting patterns we use to make life bearable, the logical progressions, the sensible happenings, the little routines, all were swept away in a wild confusion of jangling dissonant sounds and fierce unfamiliar shapes. When I looked at my surroundings, the mundane little houses, the washing lines and net curtains, they did not seem real. They were nothing, nothing – simply a pathetic attempt to impose a paltry order on the unthinkable. I could feel tears, sticky and warm, on my cheeks and the houses shimmered in a haze. My legs still carried me but I didn't know how.

When I reached the car I sank into the seat and let my head rest gratefully on the steering wheel. It was some minutes before I felt composed enough to drive off.

I bought myself some whisky in the village and consumed about half the bottle and some ham and pickle for lunch. Rook's Cottage was as silent and soulless as a box. There was a letter from Tyrrell, cheerful, chatty, wishing me well, expressing pleasure at Elise's visit, full of news about college and the academic rat race. Halfway through I put it down and forgot about it. It was like reading pages found discarded in a railway carriage. It had some curiosity value but apart from that it was just a jumble of words, references I could not understand, names and places that meant nothing. I never finished it. I sat at the kitchen table and stared into my empty glass. The quiet was oppressive, and I stood up to switch on the news on the radio. Just as I rose I experienced a horrible shock as a tall figure passed the window with long, rapid strides. He must have moved very quickly for I was still staring at the window when I heard a soft knock and the sound of the outer back door opening.

It was Holz. I had backed up against the cooker defensively at the sound of the door – my own depressed and fearful thoughts had made me afraid of my visitor. When I saw who it was I felt sharply aware of how foolish I must look, but could think of nothing face-saving to say. I need not have worried. It was as though nothing had passed between us. The sad aquiline features were completely neutral, disinterested and composed.

'I'm sorry to disturb you,' he said. 'This is my afternoon to do the garden here. Will that be alright?'

'Yes, yes . . . of course.'

'I tried to tell you, but—'

'Yes, yes, that will be fine.'

He gave a quaint, Germanic bow of the head, acquiescent though far from deferential, and retired through the back door. I saw him go into the garden shed and emerge with a rake and barrow. I watched him for a few moments, mesmerised by his presence there, moving so composedly and deliberately about the small patch, his eyes and apparently his thoughts on his work, silent through the glass.

His presence made me feel that I should at least appear to be gainfully occupied, so when I had washed up my few things I went into the sitting room with my books. As I sat there it clouded over outside and I began to wonder when Elise would return. Funny how changes in the light affect the mood. With darkness we dig in, draw together and keep close, with the light we are filled with initiative and enterprise. With those few clouds over the sun my thoughts were with other people. I needed them about me, I wanted to be reassured of their presence and their relationship with me, to know that there was not just me, and Holz, alone in this clammy brown countryside.

At about a quarter to four there was a rap on the front door and I answered it to find Ambrose Austen on the step. I could not imagine what had brought him to Rook's Cottage after our last encounter, and my dialogue with Holz was still so fresh in my mind that just to look at this dapper young man made my scalp crawl.

'Aren't you going to ask me in? Looks like rain.' He brushed past me into the hall. He wore an impeccably cut gabardine trench coat, and with the collar turned up and his hands thrust deep in his pockets he looked like one of those smug Elizabethan dandies or royal favourite, smirking from the frame of his ruff.

'What do you want?' I asked rudely.

'Happened to be passing, taking a look at the scene of the crime, you know.'

'No!' What in God's name could he mean, the scene of the crime?

'Well, prowling round the village, that's all.'

'Oh.' Silly of me, for a moment I thought – never mind what I thought but it had an army trampling over my grave.

'I thought I'd let you know,' he went on, 'that I've uncovered one or two surprises vis-à-vis the Dukes girl story.'

'You amaze me.'

'You're sceptical and scared, aren't you, Michael, a very tricky combination,' he said, the little bastard. 'I don't know how you do it. I take it you're not interested in an exclusive preview, then?'

'No. If that's all you came for, you can leave.'

'Not just the teensiest bit curious?'

The look on my face must have been ample reply for he shrugged.

'At any rate it may or may not please you to know that that isn't why I called.'

'"He only does it to annoy", eh?'

'If you like. No, the reason I dropped by was purely practical. I wondered if you, as a man of letters, had ever heard of a fellow called Latham.'

'In connection with what?'

'He's top academic brass who turns a bright commercial penny by doing whodunit-type enquiries into historical mysteries, you know the kind of thing.'

'Jack Latham. Yes, I know him, or know of him. He's clever.'

'Sounds like damning with faint praise. Intellectual lightweight, is he?'

'I've no idea. I've only met him twice, at academic parties. I meant simply that all I know of him is that he's considered clever.'

'I wanted to approach him on certain matters of presentation, I'd quite like to quote him, actually.'

'But he deals purely in hypothesis.'

'Exactly.'

'I see.' If this obnoxious young man stood near me for much longer I was going to do something violent and regrettable. I said tersely: 'Jack Latham's on a sabbatical at present doing another book. I imagine you could get him through his college. And don't tell me a hack like you isn't perfectly capable of tracking down a helpless don.'

'I didn't say I was incapable of tracking him down.' Austen's voice was silky. 'I wanted an impression – an opinion.'

'And are you satisfied that you have one?'

'Yes. He sounds the man for the job.'

'What precisely is the job?'

'I thought you'd never ask. We – my paper – want him to do his stuff on the Ballacombe story.'

'You want to re-create it – to surmise, just for the sake of your bloody readers' prurient interest?'

'Something like that, though I'd take issue with your choice of words. Don't rubbish my readers – it's the great British public you're talking about. For "prurient" I'd say "public". Public interest—'

'The usual excuse.'

'And as for surmise, I believe I'm well past that.'

'Into the vicious and unfounded allegation stage, are we?'

This time I'd hit home. There was no smile as he said: 'Don't underestimate me, Mr Bowater. I certainly don't underestimate you. There's plenty you're keeping to yourself.' My face must have showed something for he went on, 'Oh yes. Professor of English, student of human nature, right? But we sniffers-out of stories get to be pretty hot on human nature too. Our vulgar obsession with sex and death and the link between the two isn't just sound commercial sense, it's the fruit of experience.'

I stared at him, the stare I usually reserved for recalcitrant students, but Austen was an altogether tougher proposition. He was, literally, doorstepping me, and not about to go till he'd said his piece.

'I've come across the Marion Dukes type more often than you've had hot dinners. Sexy, manipulative, good actress, a tease. A you-know-what sort of teaser too, only I'm too much of a gentleman to use that word to a professor.' He lifted an eyebrow.

I tried to stifle and contain the inner boom of shock. Not at the coarse expression he'd forborne to use, but at what he was implying. It was part of my defence to speak, though this would have been the moment not to talk.

169

'For Christ's sake, you make out you're so worldly – young girls experiment.'

'Oh, they do, they do . . . And some go one way, what you might call the usual way. And some go the other. And for those ones there's no going back. Is there? They're the vulnerable ones. They're vulnerable to the experimenters. To the Marions.'

'I'm afraid you've lost me completely.'

He dipped his head, pretending silent laughter. But when he next looked at me his face was mean.

'Let's all hope justice will be done, Mr Bowater.'

'God.' The word justice coming from him was sickening. Suddenly all I wanted was for him to be gone. 'Get out.'

'Sure. I only dropped by for your opinion of Latham. Thanks for that, and maybe we'll wash up against each other again one of these days.'

'I hope not.'

'I've had some other ideas while I've been down here. Something for the women's page. A makeover.' I must have looked blank. 'That's giving someone a new look. There's a few could benefit from our fashion editor down here, make a nice little spread.'

He got behind the wheel and rolled the window down, his hand on the ignition key. 'That Susan Deller. Could be a looker, don't you reckon? But no idea. She'd scrub up nicely given the right advice.' He started the engine. 'But then she's not bothered.'

We exchanged a look, his amused, mine furious, and he was gone, with a just audible: 'Look out for the story.'

As I turned, shaking with anger, I heard a faint sound from the kitchen, the spurt and rattle of the tap running in the sink. Mrs Payne? It wasn't her day. Too upset already to be anxious I swung open the door, which had been ajar, and came face to face with Holz, dressed in his gardening overalls, filling a bucket at the sink.

'Good afternoon.' He lifted the bucket out easily and stood there with it hanging heavily from his long, strong hand. He was impassive. Yet he must have heard everything. 'I've about finished. I'll just clear up and be on my way.'

'You heard Mr Austen?'

He affected not to hear and made for the door. Frozen with fear I watched him go. There seemed to be nothing to say, and yet so much to communicate: feelings of guilt, of sorrow, of friendship. As it was, all I could do was stand there in that plain, dour little kitchen, and stare through the window at the tall, lonely figure moving about his tasks in the garden, as though by keeping my eyes on him I could impart something of my terrible sense of tragedy. He was so calm, and yet it seemed to me that the quality of his calm had changed. Before it had been reserved and gentle, now I thought I saw, in my panic and anxiety, an iron resolve in those hands, in the bend of that back, the angle of the head. What might this man not do after what he had heard?

Ashamed of my own timidity I opened the kitchen door and went out into the garden. Holz was emerging from the shed, having deposited some tools. He had put a mac on over his overalls, and was obviously about to go.

'Mr Holz – Jan –'

He looked at me, his face a polite question mark. So different from the relaxed almost animated man I had talked to in the cottage that morning.

'I don't know what to say,' I muttered, stating the obvious.

'Say nothing then.'

'But what will you do?'

'Do?' He seemed surprised; then thoughtful: 'I'm not sure.'

'You see now why I was anxious – about my dream. I'm truly terrified in case it comes true.'

'That dream, ah . . .' Extraordinarily, he gave me a sad smile. 'That dream won't come true. If I were you I should go back to London and not worry yourself about it any more.'

I should have felt relief, but I didn't. On the contrary it seemed that a door had been closed quietly and firmly in my face, just as I had been about to see the answer to my questions. I had blundered this far and met with no resistance, now the time had come for me to be excluded.

As I stood there clumsily, Holz turned and left. If I'd had the strength I would have leapt on him and forcibly restrained him, *made* him listen to me. But as it was, I was rooted to the spot. I have had dreams where people eluded me, where faces melted away as I was about to recognise them, and where familiar street corners turned into unfamiliar streets. But this was worse, far worse. The sense of exclusion was bleaker than any nightmare. I was quite certain that the events of the past half an hour presaged the killing that I knew was to come, and yet I was powerless to prevent it. The odd thing was that the characters in my macabre scenario seemed to have taken on a prescience of their own. Austen had been smug, self-contained, Holz quietly decisive: it was as though time had zig-zagged crazily and only I, poor frightened academic that I was, was rushing hither and thither trying to restore logic and sanity. I did something I have never in my life felt moved to do before. I took the car, left the cottage unlocked for Elise's return, and drove down to Ballacombe church.

It was five o'clock as I passed under the prettily carved canopy of the lych-gate, and the old man who tended the graveyard was just leaving. He tipped his cap to me and his bright little eyes scanned me curiously.

'Vicar's not there,' he said.

'I'm not looking for him.'

'Oh well, door's unlocked, then. I'll be saying good-night.'

He disappeared, still casting glances over his shoulder to see what I was about. I walked quickly in the direction of the church path. I was filled with an atavistic urge to be there in the still, cool twilit church with those staunch doors shut behind me, and I began to run.

Once inside, I stopped and walked slowly, quietly up the aisle and into one of the pews at the front directly beneath the pulpit. I felt watched, not by eyes but by inanimate objects. The accumulated solemnity of hundreds of years looked gravely down upon me, a miserable sinner, as I knelt there. The Bible lying open on the lectern, the towering hooded pulpit, the unlit candles like sentries on the altar, even the cool, old wood of the pew where I knelt, polished by generations of elbows, knees and hands, had seen it all before.

I suppose you could call it praying. I was certainly a suppliant, craven and desperate, but I had had no practice in addressing the Almighty since my school days and the extent of my prayer was to mutter, 'Help me, help me,' over and over again.

The odd thing was that, while I was by no means an instant convert, my belief in the subjective and auto-suggestive powers of prayer was confirmed. When after five minutes I rose stiffly and began to make my way out of the church, I did feel better. Though exhausted, the world seemed a little less menacing. Which goes to show how foolishly willing people are to believe in what they wish were so.

Twelve

E lise was not late back, but I'd already gone to bed and was lying there reading, or at least staring at a book, when I heard the slow purr of the Dellers' Jag in the lane. It stopped, with that wonderful dying fall that expensive cars have, the passenger door clunked shut and I heard Elise making her soft, pretty farewells. I could picture her standing there, the perfect guest, watching and smiling in the dazzle of the headlamps until Arnold had turned laboriously in the narrow space and was heading back.

She appeared in my bedroom doorway, chatty and vivacious. It was clear she'd had a good day. Her ego was boosted, she thrived on attention.

'I think I might stay a little longer,' she said, as she slipped off her earrings and unbuttoned her blouse. 'Would that be a problem?'

I hesitated, and she added at once: 'I promise not to be a nuisance.'

That, of course, made me feel a bastard.

'Of course you can stay. What about work?'

'I have a sin to confess –' She turned to me as she stepped out of her skirt, then crossed the landing to put the clothes away – she was meticulous about such things.

'Really?'

'I've taken a whole week off – just in case. So now I can stay if you'll have me.'

'Fine.' I was still being ungracious but on this occasion she chose not to pick me up on it.

'Thank you, Michael.' She slipped her negligée over her petticoat and went to the bathroom, saying over her shoulder: 'You won't know I'm here . . .'

In truth, I barely did. This was because she spent almost all her time at the Dellers, who had taken her up in a big way. It shamed me to admit that I was jealous. It was I who had got to know them first, who had introduced her to them, and now I was being left out in the cold. Left in peace was how they would all see it, I realised that. I was being perverse.

Also, I had the peculiar idea that while she was there, nothing would happen. To me, that is. None of those mysterious visions, premonitions, insights, whatever they could be called. With Elise here, monopolising my new life and friends, she was the star and I was the bit-part player. My uniqueness, even in my own eyes, was diminished.

This attitude wasn't rational; and neither was it justified. For Elise was out most of the day, though she was always back to pour me a drink and provide something elegant (not necessarily laboured-over) for dinner. The place looked, felt and smelled nicer with her around – the flowers, the fresh coffee, her bath oil . . . Any reasonable man would have been delighted.

But something was waiting for me out there, something to which, in spite of my fear, I was magnetically drawn. I chafed, until one afternoon, the reality that was right beneath my nose jumped up and shocked me out of my preoccupation.

It was a fine day. I'd gone out for a breather in the early afternoon and because of the route I'd taken, skirting the edge of the wood, my return was down the hill at the back of the house. When I was a couple of hundred yards away

I saw two figures in the garden: Elise, and Susan. I was about to hail them when the weaselly desire to see and not be seen stopped me. I paused, moving a little to one side so that I knew (I'd stood gazing up the hill so often) that unless they were specifically looking for me I'd be masked by the apple tree.

They were standing – we'd put away the garden furniture, it was no longer warm enough to sit out – but quite close together. Elise was talking, I could tell by the angle of her head, and Susan was looking slightly away, and down, arms folded. As I watched Elise moved fractionally closer and Susan too turned as if responding to something that had been said. Now, something told me, was the moment to call Elise's name, to advertise myself, to break whatever spell they were under. But I didn't. I held my breath and continued to stare, aware now that I was spying.

Susan dropped her arms to her sides, but I could tell, more than see, that her fists were clenched. And from that I could picture her expression and what Elise would do in response.

Her hand drifted up to the girl's cheek and rested there in a gesture that was both elegant and tender. A gesture which I had never seen before and which made my ears ring and my stomach lurch with jealousy. Not the possessive testosterone rush of my reaction to James, but a sharp wound to the heart, bleeding bitterness like poison through my system.

There was no more to it than that. No embrace, no kiss, not even a reciprocal caress from Susan. But they held the position just long enough for the knife to turn, slowly. Then Elise walked back into the house. After a few seconds Susan followed, her arms wrapped tightly about her chest again, as if in pain. I was as sure as I could be that what I had witnessed was a rejection of some kind, or at least an acknowledgement of hopelessness, but that only made it worse. I writhed under my wife's magnanimity, and the obvious feeling between the two of them. All that love directed at and deflected by her, whereas I . . .

When I came in through the back door I could hear music from the front room. I went through and found Elise sitting on her own, looking at the newspaper. She looked up as I entered and smiled – a smile of real gentleness and warmth, which might have been for me, but which I interpreted as the legacy of her meeting with Susan.

'Hallo . . .' She folded the paper and put it down. 'Where did you go?'

'Not far. Up round the edge of the wood.'

I tried to detect a hint of self-consciousness or guilt as she realised the path I would have taken, and the view it afforded of the back garden; but there was none.

Instead, she said: 'Susan was here, you just missed her.'

'Oh.'

'It was a nice afternoon so we walked back together. Don't look so sceptical, Michael, perhaps I am being converted to country ways . . . Anyway, I should not have invited her in. She has this little crush on me, and . . .' She made a gesture that was half-shrug, half-dismissal. 'It's horrid to hurt young feelings.'

'And so often.' I didn't even try to disguise my sarcasm. But once again she either didn't notice or chose to ignore it.

'I am going to make some strong coffee.' She rose and as she went past me she brushed my cheek almost absentmindedly with her hand, in a pale imitation of the caress she had bestowed on Susan.

There was a mirror above the mantelpiece, and I could see myself in it: tightlipped, angry, preoccupied. It occurred to me for the first time that so many people could not be wrong, and that it was only with me that my wife was cold. That it was not love she was incapable of, but me she was incapable of loving.

The following night, having remained in all day and made various phone calls connected with her return to work, she went out after supper.

'Girl-talk,' she said. 'Marjorie wants me to be a clothes consultant and help her to refine the contents of her wardrobe.'

Poor Marjorie, I thought. She won't have a thing left.

'I shan't be long!'

But she was. At the first sound of the car turning into the lane I switched the light out, I didn't want to be caught staying awake for her at a quarter to one in the morning.

Ironically, seeing the dark house she must have been loath to disturb me for the car stopped well before reaching the cottage and I heard neither voices nor the door closing before the rising note of it reversing away.

After a brief silence I heard her let herself in at the side door and then pause. Two taps: she had removed her muddy shoes. Water splashed for an instant: she was washing her hands. I heard the smooth slide of the china cupboard as she took out a cup and then the splash again as she filled it. Footsteps on the lino; the click of the light going off; a softly creaking hush as she made her way softly up the narrow strip of carpet in the centre of the stairs, not wanting to disturb me.

I had not realised how tense I was until I got out of bed and met her. I had bent the spine of the book by the unconscious pressure of my fingers, and my neck was aching and rigid with listening. I opened the door and confronted her on the dark landing.

It was like looking at a reflection of myself. If I had hoped for some relief through contact with my wife I was cruelly disappointed. Her face was white and drawn and her eyes met mine with a dull sadness as though she had come through hell but was too tired to make anything of it.

'I have something I must tell you.' She took the words out of my mouth. I nodded dumbly and stood back so that she could enter my room.

Inside, we perched on the edge of the bed like homesick schoolchildren, Elise clutching her cup of cold water in two hands like a talisman. I thought, how ironic, she has come into my room at last, and willingly and yet I could no more touch her now than touch a corpse.

'Well?'

'I've been at the Dellers.'

'I know.'

'Susan was there again. We talked for ages.' She stopped, staring in her mind's eye at whatever had happened between them. But I did not prompt her and in a minute or so her voice, deathly quiet like the rustle of dead leaves, went on.

'She told me everything. About herself, and what she's done. You see, she killed that Dukes girl.'

I gasped. If Elise had told me she herself had done it, I could not have been more shocked. It took all my energy simply to digest the information, and I was still grappling with it as Elise went on, quiet and monotonous as though reading a prepared speech.

'I told you she preferred women. Well she's always been the same and it's isolated her terribly. She's always been big and awkward and at her school in Leeds she found the more she strove for popularity the fewer friends she had. She began to make real advances, desperate advances and then to bitterly regret it. Some parents of other girls complained and Arnold was furious. He's always loved her and stood by her and refused to believe the innuendos. If only Susan herself could have explained to him, but she's built herself a tall prison without any window and she's going to rot in it . . .'

She faltered for a moment, her voice catching on a dry little sob, and then went on: 'If she had had the words to tell him he could have understood and helped – his love and trust are absolute – but she didn't and he was too loyal to accept it from other people. So there they are, two magnificent people letting each other go to the devil and poor dear Marjorie in between, hoping to rationalise it all with common sense and good cooking. So . . . Arnold retired and brought them down here, thinking that the country would protect them all, that it would neither ask him, nor tell him, what his secret was. Susan loves gardening, and the countryside, and she spent literally months with no other friends except Holz while she helped him to create that quasi-Versaille up there.' Good old Elise. Her fastidious taste coloured even this story.

'Apparently,' she went on, 'Susan met Marion Dukes at a garden centre outside Exeter, not in the village at all, isn't that cruel? She went there with Marjorie to buy bedding plants and Marion was there with another fifth-former doing some kind of project on how the place was run. Susan claims they hit it off at once, that there was a strong mutual attraction but reading between the lines it's pretty obvious the girl was a flirt and a tease. She was a knowing little school nymphet, she got Susan's number right away and played her along. To make matters worse Marjorie, poor soul, positively encouraged the whole thing because she was so delighted to see her poor, awkward, misunderstood daughter actually hitting it off with a girl whom she considered to be thoroughly 'normal'. She invited Marion up to tea, got to know the parents and generally made herself agreeable. She must have wondered why things never progressed, why other girls didn't come on the scene, why Susan never went out anywhere with them, even why no boys ever materialised. In fact, to all intents and purposes the friendship came to nothing. That was what Marjorie thought, and that's why she was never even remotely suspicious when Marion disappeared. What happened was that Marion led Susan on in ways she knew would be interpreted by Susan as advances. Susan plunged in and became thoroughly involved and they began to meet clandestinely. Thoroughly guilty and confused, but in too far to escape, Susan lied that she'd lost interest in the girl. They used to meet at weekends and in the evening, go for long walks and continue with what to Marion was just a bit of a lark, to Susan nothing less than a serious affair. It's quite pathetic the way she talks about it, she says she'd never found anyone who understood her so well, who wasn't repelled by her and so on. She still sees it even now as some kind of grand passion when in fact it was a rather sordid exercise in experimental sex and manipulation of one personality by another.'

She looked at me for an instant, bleakly, but just as I was about to stretch my hand to touch hers she looked away again as though, when she was speaking, she could not bear to watch her own pity and horror reflected on another face.

'Of course the inevitable downward spiral began. Marion wasn't involved, didn't care, soon became bored with Susan's protestations of affection, probably genuinely unsettled by them. The time had come for a break but Susan was unable to make it a clean one. She pleaded and begged and demeaned herself and they went on seeing each other until Marion, in a fit of petulant rage, told her she'd tell everyone about the affair unless Susan stopped pestering her. Susan told me she understood how Marion must have felt – imagine! – but that she simply couldn't let her go. They had a physical struggle – quite violent – Susan's actually still got some scars on her temple under her hair. Of course she was much bigger and stronger than

Marion and she was desperate. All that powerful emotion and desire, and sheer frustration suddenly given its head. She killed the girl while trying to keep her.'

Elise gave a shaky sigh, as though, having said the worst, it was now a little easier to go on.

'She says she began by simply trying to restrain her, and then realised that, meeting with resistance, she was beginning to fight. The sensation went to her head – she got wilder and wilder and was still hitting and tearing at the girl after she'd died. Then, she was panic-stricken, wild with remorse. She ran to Holz.'

'Of course.' The story made perfect, horrible sense. The picture came into focus, the wheel came full circle. 'Of course, she ran to Holz. And all this time, he's known.'

'Yes . . .' Elise looked at me quizzically, uncertain about my reaction and what it meant. But I was impatient now. 'Go on.'

'As a matter of fact Holz knew all about Susan and the Dukes girl. He didn't like Marion. He had no cause to – she was one of those girls who just had to meddle, to see what would happen if. He had been doing a caretaking job at the school and one night she'd made a bit of a pass at him. He'd ignored her so she'd retaliated by spreading the idea he'd made a pass at *her*. Not an accusation, you understand, nothing worth proving or disproving, just a little fuel to the fire of prejudice. He could foresee the way things would go. I think he truly loves Susan – in the way he loves his garden, his flowers, his animals – to him she's life in its unspoilt form, something completely untarnished, whole and trusting. He never hesitated when she told him what had happened. Do you want to know what he did?'

'Yes.' I was absolutely fascinated. Any repugnance I might have felt was swamped by my mounting excitement and my curiosity to know every last detail.

'Well, he was very organised,' said Elise, 'very Teutonic,

you could say. He incinerated the clothes in the garden incinerator out here in the shed.'

'What here? In Tyrrell's shed?'

'Yes. Then he got Susan to help him bury the body.'

'Where?'

'They hauled it between them up to that wood at the top of the hill. It's just a tangle of brambles but they pushed and buried her right in the middle.'

'On the old church path.'

'That I wouldn't know about. Apparently the place has some local significance, it's supposed to have a hex on it.'

'Oh yes.' There must have been a craziness in my voice for she looked at me sharply.

'So that was it. She'd told me everything, and what was I to do? In God's name, Michael, what *am* I to do?'

'You will do nothing, as ever, my darling,' I replied cruelly, 'but carry on in your own elegant way and put it all down to experience. You managed to stay on at the Dellers after hearing all this, didn't you? You managed to drink gin, and eat dinner and exchange chit-chat, didn't you? Don't you worry, it need mean nothing more than a ripple on the surface of your pre-dinner cocktail.'

She rose, white-faced, and I did too to show how unshocked, how strong I was. Her face for the first time looked hard, its beauty pinched and drawn with humiliation, but she said nothing and it was I who left the room, brushing past her and not looking back.

I got into the car in a state of high expectancy, of exhilaration even. It wasn't until I reached the turning into the main road that I paused to ask myself where I was bound. It was only a brief pause and the question soon answered: to Holz's house. I drove like the wind, like the lunatic which at that moment I was. I sang, loud and crazy for the world to hear, I rolled the windows down, and pressed my horn to tell those hunched, secretive dark fields that I was coming to get them.

At the bottom of Ballacombe High Street a big dark figure, pale-faced in the headlamps, stood with arm uplifted in greeting, or farewell, or to stop me. It was Cyril Thorne but I was gone by so quickly that his startled expression was no more than a faint scribble on the night air.

The roar of the engine grated over the silence of the deeply sleeping council estate. I leapt from the car outside Holz's house and yelled, 'I'm here!' at the top of my voice. But it was quiet as the grave, no one there. As I turned to run back I saw a man blocking my way on the path. One of the locals, trying to be a police-man. I almost knocked him over and, getting back into the driver's seat, heaved the car round and set off back the way I had come. I was possessed with enormous energy, I could *make* things happen. I would, I would be there, I would race against time and win. And now, if Holz was not in his house I knew where he would be.

I left the car at Rook's Cottage and ran like a deer along the lane, swallowing up the ground, with no sense of tiredness. As I ran I became conscious of company, not visible company but sounds, vibrations, impressions on the air all around me like a mosaic in the darkness. Arms linked with mine, feet pounded before and behind, soft faces brushed my cheek and hands patted and pushed to help me along. I came to the lighter patch where the high hedge was broken by the gate and turned with a pulsating feeling of excitement.

There they were, two blacker shapes against the night grey of the sky, one taller than the other. As I clambered over the gate they drew together, I could hear the sounds of their struggle and could see the smaller one, Austen, bending back under the onslaught of Holz. I would not call out, I would stop them myself, bodily. There was nothing I could not do.

The lumpy plough presented no problem to me this time, I was sure-footed and quick. In an instant I had grabbed Holz's sleeve. His arm felt thin and hard through the material, but he did not resist.

I looked down at the smaller figure lying curled on the ground, one hand caught beneath the cheek as it fell, like a child asleep. All I could think was: Had I won?

'You've killed him?'

'No,' said Holz. He sounded terribly tired. 'I have not killed him.'

Elation – I knelt by the figure on the ground and as I did he added softly: 'I have killed her.'

It was Susan Deller. So incredulous was I that I put my face against hers, feeling her features like a blind person on a dig with my lips, nose, my fingers, even my eyelashes. She smelt nice – clean and wholesome as bread, or something good that grew out of this rich soil, as though she was meant to be there. I thought, This is an odd experience, to be with someone who has only seconds before met with violent death, as though you could ask: 'What does it feel like? Where are you now?' She felt warm and the night air cold. I instinctively drew her jacket more snugly around her before standing up.

Now all the elation had gone. For Susan, the innocent, the lovely, the unspoilt, had been killed. By Jan Holz, who stood next to me, carefully wiping that knife which had carved such beautiful things. And now done this.

'Why?' I asked.

He looked at me, his head turning towards me in the dark. His voice was very tender, almost loving. It came out to me like the hand of friendship and sympathy. I could feel no hatred for him. '"For each man kills the thing he loves," your poor poet said. And he was right. I should rather pay myself twice over than see her pay. Besides – there was even a hint of a smile in his voice – 'everyone expects me to.'

I left him standing there in the dark and walked back to the cottage. And all the way they were with me – the people, from the past and the future. The people who had shown me, who had directed my steps and my eyes, who had run beside me in the night, urging me on. The people whose voices I had heard, down across the years, when I had been standing in Ballacombe Wood, perhaps on the very spot where Marion Dukes was buried. I knew now that they would be with me always. There was no shrugging them off, or ignoring them. They might stand back awhile as I went through the motions of my life, but they would be back. When I was alone. When it was dark. Then they would rustle forward out of the shadows, out of the frightening caves at the back of my mind, to show me the things I would rather not see, and whisper in my ear of happenings I would rather not hear of. And all my life I would bear the guilt, and the loneliness, for only I would know.

I did not reach Rook's Cottage. I sat down in the cold, prickly darkness at the side of the lane and wrapped my arms about my bunched-up knees. No more responsibility for me, I thought. I shall wait here till somebody finds me. When it's daylight.